These Corridors
(Crime Thriller)

Sudha Sikrawar

BLUEROSE PUBLISHERS
India | U.K.

Copyright © Sudha Sikrawar 2024

All rights reserved by author. No part of this publication may be reproduced, stored in a retrieval system or transmitted in any form or by any means, electronic, mechanical, photocopying, recording or otherwise, without the prior permission of the author. Although every precaution has been taken to verify the accuracy of the information contained herein, the publisher assumes no responsibility for any errors or omissions. No liability is assumed for damages that may result from the use of information contained within.

BlueRose Publishers takes no responsibility for any damages, losses, or liabilities that may arise from the use or misuse of the information, products, or services provided in this publication.

For permissions requests or inquiries regarding this publication, please contact:

BLUEROSE PUBLISHERS
www.BlueRoseONE.com
info@bluerosepublishers.com
+91 8882 898 898
+4407342408967

ISBN: 978-93-5989-392-1

Cover design and Illustraions: Jameela Kagzi
Typesetting: Namrata Saini

First Edition: January 2024

Dedicated

To my father who is still with me and I felt that during the writing of this book he was sitting with me and presenting his logical thoughts to my mother. And at the same time, I dedicate this book to today's young generation, in whom somewhere I see the commitment to take Hindi literature forward and maintain its level too.

Commitment seems to be symbolic, but still it is present somewhere.

These corridors

It is good to have an open mind but don't be so open that you fall into a trap.

Groucho Marx

Preface

Does this also happen? Usually, I do not write any novel or story on crime if something happens with us or our closed one then it's our responsibility to put light on these issues or problems. But on social issues there are definitely questions in my written story or novel. These social issues also come under the category of crime in a way. Such an incident had happened in front of me in which the criminal was present in front of the victim all the time posing himself as her loved one. "That Second Street Of Babu Maam", which I had written a book on a true incident, I had to face a strange reaction from the people.

Leaving aside the matter of people, my best friend had said - "Can this happen?", How can someone be so stupid ? One of my best friend said after reading this book of mine -" Go and cremate this book in the river Ganges, perform its last rites, what have you written-nonsense. "

That friend of mine told me over the phone that after reading every ten pages of this book, she had thrown the book away in frustration. Since you wrote this book and you are my friend, it was compulsory to read this book. But when the same best friend of mine got trapped in the ultimate trap of the internet, that day she admitted the fact and said - "Yes Sudha, your book, "That Second Street of Babu Maam " is actually a book based on a true incident. You have written such a crime thriller, "Which Was giving a strong message, I made a mistake to understand that book. I am very sorry for that, at that time I abused you too."

Yes, this also happens and it is happening even today, this unstoppable phenomenon has started. I had almost given up writing after completing, "That second Street of Babu Mam". Then after a long break I thought that I should write a story which was imprinted on my mind and heart since childhood. Then don't know whether I will get time or not. Finally I started penning the book and named it - **"ARNIMA"**. ARNIMA is the story of a girl as a central character, all the other characters either revolve around her or become secondary in the end. Aranima wins even after losing her entire life and the world remains as a small dot for her.

Right now when I was writing Aranima that my same friend, who had called " That Second Street of Babu Maam " a rubbish book, phoned me and said - "Now again write one more book on cyber crime story based on the true incident. Then whatever happened to her life, she narrated me on the phone and at the same time she insisted me to join Insta Gram. Though I already had an Insta account but I was barely active on it. When I joined Insta account on her saying, I was shocked to know that she had been cheated on insta and face book account since more than two years. My mind became numb. I was stunned to see such perverted form and indecent behavior of society. Not that all were like this, but few of them were using these platforms for cheating and looting money. Staying away from their loved ones, people have established a separate world of their own on Insta and Face book. Strangers became their dear ones and closed got apart ones. Strangers and foreigners started contacting on Insta and Face book then phone numbers were exchanged and then a long series of love talks would begin. The game of deceiving minds started, people do not understand what is happening to them. Some people were talking about love and some people were being shown sex videos and blackmailed by showing the same video and still it is going on now, I don't think it will stop anywhere. From sixteen year child to eighty years adult **(especially female)** were cheated. Targeted victims's bank accounts became empty. And the biggest thing was that the money was being transferred through the bank itself, yet people were hesitating to complain.

Not only common men or women got trapped in this but big officers from private sectors as well as from government sector married women and men also got trapped in this scandal named as "HONEY TRAP". After all, what is forcing we Indians need to hunt for this love on these trendy social platforms. So I am presenting "This corridor" in front of all of you, hope now you all will not repeat that this also happens, does it? Because many of us have been targeted till now, it is a different matter that they do not accept it in front of everyone due to social and family reasons.

The fashion of this slogan **'Age is just a count'** has spread like a virus in our society. Many people have asked me on Insta that if an eighteen year old boy makes a relationship with a thirty eight year old woman, then what is the harm or wrong in it? When I said that it is completely wrong. Then they argued that when an old age men can have relationships with younger women? Yes, I agreed after all, age is a number, we do not turn sixteen as soon as we are born. Gradually, growing each day one by one, we reach the point where we experience the world given by nature. Then why this age leap? Why so soon? Animals and birds also mate at time decided by nature itself? Then why can't human beings ?

It is a natural process for an eighteen year old boy to be attracted towards any woman other than his mother and sister. He is only attracted towards her body, love has nothing to do with him. The release of hormones in our body controls our behavior. But if a thirty eight year old woman establishes a relationship with an eighteen year old young man, then she becomes the reason for the ruining of that young man's life by raising a question mark on the existence of motherhood too. The tradition of living and customs of our Indian society is the most highly valued tradition in the world. In ancient times, the science behind keeping a gap of seven to eight years is that man's reproductive hormones remain active for more than sixty years, but woman are almost deprived of those hormones as soon as they reach fifty. And her complete attention is divided in her husband's family along with her parents replacing by lust with love.

After fifty years, lust has no place in her life. When nature has determined life sequentially, taking it from one to two and then to three, then in reality age is just a count, at least we Indians should maintain the dignity of this count.

This reference definitely touches the background of my book somewhere. I have answered this question hoping to satisfy everyone's query on instagram.

While I was penning this book, there were many reports of looting online. But neither any law was implicated to punish these criminals nor was it being thought of. When Only a common man was being targeted, the Government didn't even think to legislate against these cyber crimes until it becomes prevalent.

When the reputation of famous leaders of America and Britain was damaged through Artificial Intelligence, only then did the law awaken. Now laws are being made to stop cyber crime, but this crime is never going to stop. Today the world is in our fist and we are in the grip of the of the world.

The new dimension of development that the dormant minds of the youth have got due to the online system is continuously leading them towards criminal activities. Solving which has now become a challenge. Like a mere hello of illiterate youth of Jamtara makes people helpless victim. At this time, under the influence of the rituals received from human birth and the style of living of today's environment, a situation of a great war has arisen.

Now listen to the incident that happened with my friend which turned her life upside down. These crimes will never end as long as this universe exists but surely will manifest in different forms. Hear her story in my words.

Sudha Sikrawar

The First letter

(AGE IS A NUMBER)

My Dear Papa (father)

Greetings

How are you? Today I missed you a lot. And those letters which were written by you I am missing much more then you. Actually they were not only letters but lessons of life learned from tiny things and incidents. When I was staying in the hostel far away from home, I used to receive letters from you every week. My friends used to wait for your letters more than me and read your letters before I did. They were not only letters but weekly Newspaper. From household to Social matters, like discussions among your friends at the betel shop of the crossroads, lions coming to our fields and many such things were thoroughly depicted in your letters. The Transformation of a lion to become a man-eater. But when the same lion tried to eat the child of a laborer working in the fields, that woman killed the lion from her axe. The lion which could not be killed by the expert hunter was killed by an ordinary laborer woman, this was the power of a mother's love. Whether it's an inland letter or an envelope was always became short to explain your detailed incidents. And I used to get very annoyed after reading your exaggerated letters, which I thought was not needed. According to my point of view a letter should limit to precise information only.

I used to get very angry with you because all my friends would make fun of me and say that Vedika's father's newspaper has arrived. But at the same time they also said that no matter how long the letters are but they increase our general knowledge.

But I always replied to you in few lines asking about your and family member's health at home

Everything else is fine, rest in the next letter.

Your daughter Vedika.

Even today I was remembering those letters which have imprinted on my memories as if it happened yesterday. Today I think those letters were not just lines rather they were hiding a very important message describing current ongoing social issues. You used to explain to me very lovingly that you should be aware and observant of what is happening around. In those detailed letters you used to emphasize on socio-political matters of our country as well as foreign countries to become a vigilant and responsible citizen.

You always complained to me that I gave you very brief answers. But today you might get tired of reading my letters, perhaps I will not be able to write you the entire saga because it is endless. Today it is an era of Insta, Face book, email and Whats aap, these are such platforms where every person is beating its own drum. Someone is dancing, someone is singing and even someone is getting naked too. In the morning, we all look first at our mobile instead of praying to God. In your days very few people were getting BP and Sugar like lifestyle diseases but now a day's people have become venerable to these diseases more often. These days the evolved technologies and social platforms have trapped the human kind and made them victims of early age heart attacks, mental disorders like depression, anxiety and dementia and has become the major reason of vision loss too.

GIANT foreign companies have entered and are selling their brands and we buy them like fools and are very happy that we are wearing branded clothes. And we had lost our charm of shopping for our festivals like Holi, Deeval, Raksha Bandhan and ied etc. These High branded Companies had taken away our happiness which we used to feel in very small things. Now

Show-off has become synonym of happiness. These big GIANT only decide fashion trends for us keeping their target to get more profit from customers. We have no option left for us to choose whatever we like to wear and eat. This is the world of dominance of marketing over basic necessities. Basic needs have a new line which can be described as a luxurious life style. Now we have collected heaps of waste cloth in our homes. I was also walking on the same track before I realized these facts. Simplicity has been lost.

Earlier people used to survive by doing small jobs in their homes. And living was done very easily because the needs were very less; it was not a trend of fashion that time. Now everyone goes out and earns money. Papa, not only out of town but also out of the country. Some are going to Canada, some to England and some to America. Even the elite class of our country is also working in other countries. Because there is a lot of money in foreign countries, people have gone and settled there and old parents are left behind here for which old age homes are being opened in our country like India....

In big cities of India, elderly people living alone and getting murdered. When they die of illness or they leave this world after completing a certain age, their neighbors give them their last rites. The children sitting abroad bids his last farewell by making a video call because they don't have time, the tickets are also expensive. Who would spend money unnecessarily, they are already dead, will they come back after our arrival and these are the arguments of the sons settled abroad.

As these foreign Countries entered and started to expand on our land of India resulting in the initiation of privatization in all sectors. As a result to grab a good Job opportunity youth started to migrate from small cities and rural areas to major cities. This privatization has ruined our traditional joint family system and left everybody almost alone. In order to fulfill our need and greed youth started to migrate in foreign countries also creating a large vacuum in the heart of their loved ones who are left by them.

The flagrant example of this is PUNJAB.

In order to achieve the ambitions of getting successful and ample of money youth have lost their emotions to such an extent that now they feel their parents are burden for them.

My dear papa recently someone had shared an incident on instagram that shook me deep inside stated that an elderly woman died and survived by two sons, both lived in America. The younger son reached his mother's funeral and made a video call to let the elder son see his mother for the last time. The elder son said on the video call to him that you have incurred a lot of expenses, when father dies I will come and the expenses will be equalized. After listening to this father locked himself in the room and shot himself so that the expenses of his sons could be saved.

Foreigners come to India to do research on learning the art of living together from Indian families. But we have lost our belief in our own tradition and culture.

You might be wondering why am I not coming on the main issue. But I have learned form you only to understand the central or main issue, we should always study the surrounding exponents also. This approach always enables us to understand the centralized issue to find the better solution. And these small things which we ignore become important issues and even bring storms in our life.

A similar tempest also came in my life which emptied all the space and created a void or desolation in my life.

In your time there were letters or telegrams. These letters used to reach from one place to another through post office. But no one had any intention to open them and read those letters. But now no one writes letters, the era of e-mail has come. E-mail means electronic mail or letter. And anyone can easily steal the information and read these e-mails, this is called hacking in English. Nothing is personal anymore, everything is public now.

Source- Material data is used to send these e-mails. And big companies of India as well as foreign Companies are charging for this data. Apart from e-mail, Face book, Instagram and Twitter accounts are on social media. In a way, these are the post offices of your times. Now scammers are robbing many people through these on line platforms.

Papa, in your time, the conversations that used to happen at the intersection or crossroads, at a betel shop or when ten or twenty people gathered, now people have started getting connected to each other on these on line platforms like What's App community, Face book and Insta gram community etc. And all the decorum has been violated on these platforms and are wasting their time in search of meaningless opportunities. Leaving our loved ones and relations far behind, we are getting connected to strangers to find love and affection. Today any simple argument on a matter can transformed to an abusive and ruthless discussion very easily showing no respect for each other.

There are some other issues also which I want to write about like wastage of food in marriage and other occasions. Apart from fashion choices, we have also become slave of their processed and junk food like Maggie, Pizza, Pasta and soft drinks and we are becoming victims of all sorts of health issues like heart attack, obesity, sugar, cancer etc. With the introduction of western world food culture, our own traditional healthy recipes and food eating habits have faded with due course of time.

Still there are many other things but I am requesting you to have patience and wait for some more time as I used to do in my childhood. Few moments more.

I know your favorite topic is still left. I will not jump to the main incident without penning about your favorites fields. Yes, I know that now your patience is also running out, just as mother and our patience used to run out in our childhood from your detailed lectures.

You always used to say that patience is the ability to endure difficult circumstances.

India is an agricultural country; there is no shortage of food and food items here. Today Pakistan is dying of hunger. Tomato is priced at Rs 800 per kg there; flour is not available at all. This is Pakistan, a fragment of the ambitions of Jinnah and Nehru. In which both of them were only concerned with their Prime Minister's chair.

Now you listen to the story of India again. In order to bring prosperity in our country technology and infrastructure should run parallel with agriculture. To expand the infrastructure we are deteriorating the situation more by misusing the agriculture land to such an extent that we could also face the scarcity of grains and water very soon. Due to improper laws and weak management farmers did not get their proper cost for their production of crops and vegetables. And being in this situation great losses farmers are forced to commit suicide. News of suicides of many small farmers are published in newspapers every day and. but they often go unnoticed by the Government.

Some farmers, out of compulsion and greed have sold their agricultural lands to house builders at throwaway prices and are still selling them. Builders have built multi-story buildings on small area of land. Would you believe that buildings have 40-50 stories, the houses built in these buildings look like chicken coops or match box? Your beloved Delhi has become a city of such numerous buildings and heaps of garbage. If you were here today, you would have cried after seeing this.

Now you listen to the condition of hospitals also. In your time there used to be only one government hospital with few private clinics. But now plenty of hospitals with latest technology and equipments have opened in small to big city. The whole medical system has turned in to brokerage business involving chemist, Laboratories and Doctors too. Even in case of normal fever many unwanted blood tests are advised. The expensive medicines have also become out of reach of poor people.

The condition of education system is even worst. The Vedic knowledge of India by which humans and the entire world learned a lot has almost disappeared today. Now schools are mere air-conditioned buildings with air-conditioned buses too. In School playgrounds have almost disappeared. Instead of tuition, there are now big coaching centers. These coaching centers have become suicide spot. The pressure to compete and fulfill their parent's dream these youths are forced to commit suicide. Students who come here to study wants to become an IAS or an engineer or a doctor. These transformations of education are like unstoppable nuclear chain reaction.

As per your ideology nation prosperity is totally dependent on education and healthy medical system. Affordability of these two systems should be maintained to benefit to every class of population. Sadly, both these things are very expensive in your society now.

There are many issues to discuss with you right now but I know you are eagerly waiting to listen for what happened to me.

Now listen to anecdote of your daughter Vedika.

It was a very sad and dark evening of 18th September 2021. I was sitting in my flat just wondering what to do and where to go? But when we are doing nothing, a lot of things are happening in our life. You know I Don't like watching TV at all. You already inculcated habit of reading newspapers to us from very childhood keeping us away from the television.

Many times TV seems very boring, they keep repeating the same news, won't these people get tired, father? Few selected media channels do pointless debate just to increase TRP of their particular channels. They invite the spoke persons of opposite parties just to ignite the current issues further giving a wrong perception to the society.

After getting consumed by these profound thoughts I realized that we are passing through the strange and endless corridors of life. And these lead us to vast spectrum of emotion that a human being can have like love, affection, betrayal, Jealousy and Greed etc.

Now the opposite sex relationship do not sustain more than a month resulting in numerous break ups in one's life span. This is called move on in English. These days some words are in vogue like me too, moving on, breakup, depression etc. Papa, there is a lot that I want to discuss with you. But I am loosing the track again.

Papa, that evening of 18th September 2021 turned into a nightmare. I don't use the Face book, Instagram quite often still I created these accounts for no reason. It was elevens at night; I was trying hard to sleep in my bed. Suddenly I heard the sound of beep on my mobile. This was an indication of the arrival of a message. Now you will be curious to know about this mobile phone. Mobile is the closet buddy to each and every one in today's world. These mobiles works exactly like computers. The computer you saw was a big box, a screen and a keyboard for typing. Nowadays mobile is a small computer which we can hold in our hand, keep in our pocket and purse. Phones that can be taken anywhere and have full features of a computer are called Android phones and I-Phone. These phones define class of today's generation also. World has become really small because of these mobiles. In these we can also avail internet facility and can see the world while walking. That means the world is now in our hand but we are far away from our loved ones. Nowadays numbers of such mobile phones are more than humans.

Sometimes even one touch on this mobile can turn one's life upside down. Today I want to narrate to you the real incident which happened because of this one touch. I don't know, One day we might be constricted in one digit only due to this over ambitious plan of digitalization of Indian government. It seems to me that this is a horrifying disaster much more dangerous than any other natural calamity. Evolution of this technology is leading us to destruction. This always become a major ground for warfare which happened in all eras.

The Great scientist Einstein has said that the third world war would be fought with weapons but the fourth one would be fought with sticks and rods.

Now coming back on my story for which you are waiting eagerly. If certain thing crossed my mind, which I need to tell you will be narrated in between the story. I know you will listen to this.

You used to say if a father will not listen to his children than who else will do? I don't know why I started looking at face book message; I was astonished to see 800 friend requests there. This reminded me of pen letters of your time. Surprisingly I accepted all friend requests on that day and just went to sleep afterwards. I was much occupied for next few days. After one week when I opened my face book account, I was stunned to see that all of them answered me and asked for my phone number. But I overlooked all except one named Doctor JOHN ROSE on 28th September 2021.From that day my story commenced on.

There was one message mentioning that I am JOHN ROSE form GREAT MENCHASTER (U.K.).May I know your name please?

I thought for sometime before connecting to him and I answered that my name is VEDIKA SINGH.

And just logged of my account and slept .I don't know under which force I opened my face book account the very next morning. A strange internal turmoil had struck my heart. Probably I was vibrating high because of magnetic pull created by the profile picture of that person.

There were several messages by John Rose, which I could not read because of shortage of time. Because of heavy schedule in school John Rose almost slipped from my mind. After six days may be on Sunday I don't exactly remember the date but it was beginning of October month. My helper at home went back around five in the evening. Papa, on some unusual evenings my heart goes in deep desolation and a dearth is being created in my heart by an unknown silence dragging me into another world. Suddenly I thought of John Rose and I opened my face book account. Oh MY God, I was surprised to see a sack filled of messages.

After a glance so many messages from John Rose a smirk flashed on my face. I am narrating a few of them, not all. Rest you can understand?

Where are you?

Why are you not answering my messages?

I am worried about your health?

Please answer immediately.

I am sending messages you like insane and I wait for your messages.

I am Thirty eight years old.

I am unmarried.

I always occupied in doing Surgeries of heart patient.

Where are you from?

Still you didn't tell?

Where do you work?

What is your age?

I am not penning all messages here just to avoid over-lengthening of this letter. But this saga is endless to wind up in one letter.

In response to his several messages, I answered in only one line that I am a citizen of India and my Name is Vedika Singh which I have already told.

Papa, if you had been with me today, this incident would never have happened. Without you this incident have cost me a lot.

You used to love lengthy discussion to get deep understanding of any matter. i exactly remember that whenever we used to travel by train, it was your first hobby to enquire about the details of passengers sitting around us. Like:

How many kids you have?

In which standard they study?

You belong to which place?

What is your profession?

What profession you want to choose when they will grow up etc.

So you used to ask so many questions to know the background of that person. You were also an expert in reading someone's face expression.

My mother used to get irritated from all this resulting in big discussion at home.

What was the need to dig so much to know about that person? Are you a Pundit, do you want to tell his future?

And you always answered very calmly that it was mandatory.

Mother asked –'"why?"

Yes, it is must to know the background of somebody to decide whether to be in touch or to be aware off.

Mother asked how to know whether someone is good or bad.

If you can read the expressions is there any need of further question?

But mother did not calm down even after hearing this and she continued muttering that who are you to read faces? In exchange to this you also gave all information about us. By taking advantage of this someone can rob our house, then only you will get satisfied with your attitude.

After hearing all this you used to keep calm with a smirk on your face but I knew very well that you are capable both understanding conversation and reading expressions too.

Now coming to the main Character of the story Doctor John Rose which you are restless to listen.

And let's deep dive in to the story-

Next day I was busy in preparing for Leh, Ladakh vacation so I didn't open my face book Account. We were group of three girls and two boys. We already did advance on line booking for hotels and flight. This was a non stop flight from Lucknow to Leh. Suddenly I look that my face book account on that night, again John Rose had sent several messages.

You didn't reply, Darling?

What do you do?

What is your Age?

Can you Share yours App Number?

I looked at the clock, it was 11 P.M.

We needed to start at three very next morning, We had a Flight at 6 A.M. Than I thought to respond him.

My Name is Vedika Singh; I have already told you this.

I reside in a city named Lucknow of India.

I am a science teacher.

I take classes of 9th and 10th Standard. Along this I also shared what's app Number.

When i was about to close my Face Book account one more message from John Rose asking – Darling what is your Country code?

I wrote down the country code and angrily said that my name is Vedika, not darling.

There was no reply on Face Book.

Then suddenly I heard a message beep sound my What's App, This was a message from an unknown number with country code + 44.

Hi! Darling this is John Rose here.

This is my number.

Please save it.

I messaged him that I am travelling to Leh tomorrow and will connect with you once I return.

Where this is placing darling?

This is a hill station in India.

Are you going alone?

No, I am going with my friends.

When will you come back?

After five days.

Will you not talk to me after reaching there?

Don't know whether mobile network will be available?

Okay, tell me what is your age?

I don't know after saying this I kept my mobile on silent mode and slept.

I woke up at 2 in the morning; I had to leave for the airport at 3 o'clock. I could not check my phone. I thought I will check my message box when I reach Leh. I was eagerly waiting for his messages.

When all five of us, me, my friend Priya, Sunita, Vinod and Praveen boarded the aircraft, John had sent twenty photographs of him on what's App. Papa, all of his photographs were so attractive that it tugged me in a temptation loop, his personality looked very dashing. He was looking 28 year old instead of 38 in his photographs..

We landed at Leh Airport at seven 'O clock in the morning. It was quite cold as I looked around I found that air port was small and also noticed the presence of numerous army men. On enquiring it was revealed that earlier this airport was built for the Army only, later it was opened for the common people also.

Two taxis of the hotel were waiting outside there and after fifteen minutes we reached our destination Hotel SANGRILA. We received a grand welcome by Hotel staff; they also greeted us with garland of flowers and white scarf. Now days this style of welcoming in all hotels has become a fashion trend. Papa you had not witnessed all this in your time. Most of the people get impressed by these trends.

We went to our respective rooms, I, Priya and Sunita shared one room, Vinod and Praveen were in the other room.

On this day we were supposed to rest in our rooms and follow guidelines advised by hotel manager to acclimatize ourselves. He also mentioned if anyone have problem in breathing then inform us on intercom. Our room was on the second floor, all our luggage was delivered to our rooms. There was no lift facility in that hotel. As we started climbing the stairs, suddenly we felt pressure and heaviness in our head. The manager was correct that body will take time to adjust with the low pressure of air at high altitude.

We did not even feel the need to change clothes there. A long range of mountains covered with snow was visible from the window. A picturesque was seen from my window, widest range of mountains covered with snow was seeming to me as if they were saying that this snow will wash away with weather but we will be there with you always.

Priya and Sunita they were fast asleep in their beds. But I was unable to sleep because of a new place. Papa, I was missing you a lot. If you were with me, you would have different vision to feel these beautiful surroundings. Don't look only at the outer beauty of these white coated mountains but also feel the arduous of the inner core too.

Be delighted to see how these rigid and hard mountains are covered with festoon of white flowers and they are trying to convince as they are always securing us.

You too are always with me as these mountains are.

I rested my head on the back of the chair and lost in your memories. Suddenly I remembered that I had to message to John Rose. I picked up the phone and started viewing at John Rose's photos; all were different from each other. It was two o'clock in the afternoon. Ignoring his country time I just messaged him-

Hello John, what are you doing?

May be you are sleeping?

I saw your photos.

All are amazing!

You look quiet young as compared to your age. You are a cardiologist, then why aren't you married yet?

I waited for his reply for some time and got upset realizing the restlessness which a stranger had created in me after such a short conversation. Papa I knew that you were sitting beside me thinking this I took a sigh of relief and leaned back on the chair and slept.

In Afternoon we had lunch, there were many dishes to eat. We could not eat much food; it felt as food and water were floating in our stomach. We all were experiencing a strange heaviness in the body.

After finishing our lunch, we got into our beds. It was 2 o'clock in the afternoon. Suddenly I thought that it must have been eight o'clock of morning in Great Manchester.

There were many messages from John Rose -

How are you?

How was your trip?

I am not married yet!

He was on line, he started chatting with me.

I asked-"Why?"

I haven't found my favorite partner yet.

Ooh.

What kind of partner do you want?

One who is good looking, educated and understands me.

But you are a handsome doctor (Cardiologist), is there not a single girl in your Greater Manchester for you?

Darling, there are many, but I haven't liked anyone yet!

Why are you calling me Darling, my name is Vedika, I have already told you.

No problem dear, I know. But I just like it saying so my darling.

How long is your vacation?

Today we didn't go anywhere but we have a plan to stay here for next four days.

Darling why didn't you go out, are you okay?

We all are fine, we will visit tomorrow.

Okay darling, I have some patients to see, I will l speak to you later.

It must be 8'O clock in the morning. Why did you come to the hospital so early?

I came to the hospital last night to perform a surgery in an emergency; I will talk to you later.

Saying ok, I hung up the phone.

The next day we were feeling a little better, Papa, we visited the entire Leh, Laddakh for four days. I heard a lot before about Nubra Valley but found only sand and camels there. Why despair arises by looking at these seas of sand creating a strange void in us Papa?

Then we visited the army area where the Kargil war took place. Kargil war was fought between India and Pakistan from 3rd May 1999 to 26th July 1999. This war is also referred to as Operation VIJAY (VICTORY DAY). So many young soldiers and officers of the Indian Army were martyred during this war. One of them was Captain Saurabh Kalia who was killed in captivity by Pakistani security forces during the Kargil war. While patrolling, he and his five other companions were captured alive and kept in captivity, where they were tortured a lot and then killed. This Kargil war started with the martyrdom of Officer Saurabh Kalia. The case against the injustice done to them is still pending in the Supreme Court. This matter should have been taken to the International Court of Justice by the Government of India, but nothing has been done till today. This is a failed action by the Government of

India. I will narrate you this story some other time, you probably won't be able to absorb because it is too harsh and painful Papa.

Here we saw the pictures of all the martyrs and also the weapons with which the war was fought. I felt a strange and shivering sensation at that moment flowing through my body.

Well, we enjoyed all tourist places as well as rafting too. I know you were very fond of travelling, if you were alive today, you would have shared all your experiences on Instagram and Facebook too. Instagram and Facebook are such social media platforms where we can express our thoughts freely. But this frankness gets buried somewhere deep down when we express our views on any issue of social or national interest. But it has no qualms in posting things and videos crossing the heights of obscenity on its platform.

Papa, I don't remember who made the Android phone. But the person who made it said just a few days ago - "I wish I had known that making Android phone would lead the world to this horrifying situation, then I would never have made the mistake. (I don't want to elaborate this matter but only I can tell you that a parallel world has been created like weeds on Instagram and other social media platforms).

We returned to our home after five days.

As soon as I arrived home, i got busy with my school work. I used to reach home from school at 2.30, P.M. Due to very busy Schedule and pending work I could not look at my phone. It was Sunday, obviously I was seeing the message of John Rose and again he had sent many of his photos. He was online that time -

Who is the other person in this photo who looks exactly like you, I asked?

This is my twin brother Joel Rose.

Why does, he look alike you.

He is also a cardiologist.

Does he also work in the same hospital?

No Dear, he is in the Scotland.

But in this photo why both of you are standing in the same hospital?

No Darling, he just came to meet me?

That is fine, if he is a visitor what is the need of wearing the same uniform of your hospital?

While returning back he wore this uniform to attend an emergency in his hospital.

You both look identical.

Yes darling, we are identical twins.

If I ever meet you, how will I recognize you?

Darling, by touch.

How is that?

If I will touch you once, then you always will be able to recognize me. That's love.

Is Joel married?

"No"

"Why?"

He will marry only when I do.

If you will not do, won't he do it too?

No, not at all darling.

You guys are very strange.

We are twins, will do the same things at the same time.

What does that mean?

Okay, leave this aside; tell me about your trip?

It was very good.

Where are you from John?

We are from Italy, darling.

Do your parents live in Italy?

Yes darling.

Why don't they live with you?

They don't want to leave Italy.

Well darling, you didn't tell anything about you but you have asked everything about me?

Oh ho, how many times I told you that my name is Vedika not Darling.

No problem Darling, now I have to rush to the hospital, will connect with you in afternoon.

What did you have in breakfast?

Coffee and Bread.

Coffee and Bread?

Is this your breakfast?

Yes darling, what do you take in breakfast? I eat this every day.

I eat nutritious breakfast like fruits, chapatti and porridge.

Okay, I'll talk to you in my lunch time; I'm getting late right now.

At exactly 7 in the evening he messaged me.

Hello darling.

Uff, how many times do I have to explain to you, my name is Vedika.

Nice darling.

Then again darling.

Yes darling.

I like to say darling.

But why?

Because I like you very much.

But you haven't seen me yet.

But i have seen your pictures.

Where?

On your DP and Facebook account.

Okay darling, please send your pictures.

Why?

I want to see you.

Okay then do a video call.

Can't do right now, will call you tonight.

He sent a voice message at mid night; that was an English love song.

Papa, lyrics of songs are-

I found a love, for me

Darling, just dive right in and follow my lead

Well, I found a girl, beautiful and sweet

Oh, I never knew you were the someone waiting for me

/
/
/
/
/

Baby, I am dancing in the dark

With you between my arms

Barefoot on the grass

Listening to our favorite song

When you said you looked a mess

I whispered underneath my breath

But you heard it

Darling you look perfect tonight

Well, I found a woman, stronger than anyone I know

She Shares my dreams, I hope that someday I'll share her home

I found a lover, to carry more than my secrets

To carry love, to carry children of our own

/

Darling, just hold my hand

Be my girl, I'll be your man

I see my future in your eyes

/

Baby I am dancing in the dark

With you between my arms

/

//

/

Darling you look perfect tonight

/

/

/

I have faith in what I see

Now I know I have met an angel in person

And she looks perfect

I don't deserve this

You look perfect tonight

After hearing this love song, I lost in another world and I slept while listening to this song. At exactly 2 o'clock in the night, I got John's voice call .Despite having a gruff voice it seemed to me like a wind chime as if some soothing music was playing near me. His style of saying hello made me speechless. It felt like someone had touched my heart today.

He became very upset after not getting any response from me – Darling, where are you?

After a long pause I replied him in very low tone.

Darling, I have been speaking for so long. Why are you not answering?

I was lost captivated by your voice.

Darling, how did you like my voice?

It is nice.

Papa, he talked to me for a long time.

Suddenly he said that you haven't told your age yet.

Papa, I remained silent for a while because I did not want to lie to him.

But I didn't want to reveal my real age to him for some unknown reason. He was thirty-eight years old and I was forty five. There was a fear that he might stop talking to me as soon as he will know my age. A cyclone of thought was spinning my heart. Once I felt like lying.

Darling, where are you?

I'm here John.

I asked you something?

Papa, I told him my age.

Hearing this he laughed and said, but you look like only thirty years to me.

I said I am eight years elder to you.

He laughed a loud and said –*"AGE IS A NUMBER FOR ME."*

Then I told him to do a video call.

He did a video call and I could not take my eyes off him, he was very handsome.

The video call got disconnected after few seconds. He told that there is a network problem.

Well, we had a long chatt that day. And after that it became routine for us .In One of these Conversation, he told that you are very beautiful and you have a British color tone. But he preferred chatting rather than calling just because of his busy schedule in hospital .Papa, this is how I saw him for the first time.

I didn't receive message from him for next three days then I messaged him. He was sad because one of his patients had died in the Hospital. I will talk to you tomorrow.

But tomorrow is Sunday; don't have you to go to Church?

Darling, I will call you after watching the football match in the evening. John was very fond of watching football matches, just like you were fond of watching wrestling.

Papa, I am very tired today.

Your daughter Vedika

Rest in next letter

******

Second letter

(I will give you my color)

My Dear Papa,

Namaste

I know that you are eagerly waiting for the next letter.

John was very fond of music, although he himself used to sing very dissonantly. But his voice never matched his face. You once told me that the personality of any person can be judged by the voice, in your research you have established that a criminal background is often associated with the voice that don't co relate with face of person. You had also processed your research paper by sending to the Medical Association. I don't know what happened to that research. But surprisingly why I could not co relate your idea to this incident. You had done a lot of research about the voice and crime which I don't remember now. This unique and Observant quality leads to this remarkable ideology.

First time I lied to him about his voice. Actually his voice was like a broken bamboo.

Long chatting and sending love songs had become a daily routine for us.

By the end of October, Priya called that she would come to me this Friday night. You know Priya, she is my childhood friend. Her husband died only after two years of her marriage. She used to visit me on weekend quiet often. These frequent meetings had made our lives much happier.

Priya came on Friday night and I got busy with her.

I received many messages from John, but I did not respond. After waiting for a long for his call I messaged him -

I am unable to talk to you today John.

Why darling, what happened?

My friend has come.

So what?

Nothing is happened, I haven't told her anything about you.

Never mind, tell her now.

No, I can't tell her, she doesn't like foreigners.

Why does she not like foreigners?

She always says that our India and the people of India are good and humble. It is the British who ruled us and looted the wealth of our country. Partition of India is the result of their dirty diplomacy. Till today, India and Pakistan are burning in the fire of their jealousy and also planted the root of terrorism in India as well as Pakistan. Once she went to America. She told me how the people of India live there? From the airport to the shopping malls, the people of there look at Indians with very strange eyes.

Well, that all has faded with time and became an old topic, now every country has its own stand i. Everyone's thinking has also changed with time.

Now our U.K. People are not like that.

Yes, but I don't think that they have changed much.

They enslaved us and ruled our country for two hundred years and looted our wealth.

Hey, leave it aside, why are you talking about politics? Send me your address.

What do you mean?

Hey I mean your mailing address or postal address.

For what ?

Want to send you some gifts.

But I didn't ask for any gift?

Darling, I want to send you a gift out of love.

Suddenly Priya came and asked whom are you chatting with ?

Instead of talking to me you are continuously chatting with someone on phone.

After saying this she snatched the phone from my hand.

Well, what is cooking between two of you?

Oh, he looks handsome and attractive.

What does he do and where he lives?

He is a doctor, lives in Great Manchester.

Means he is a foreigner. Oh why am I asking? He looks like a foreigner just by his appearance in photo.

Suddenly she paused for few seconds.

What happened Priya?

Are you really in love with him?

I don't know exactly.

So will you fly to meet him?

Yes, if he would wish.

Yes he wants; the messages are conveying this very well.

Why have you taken so long to tell me?

My mind was very uncertain because my emotions were floating.

Priya gently placed hand on her shoulder and then said don't think too much. Such opportunities do not knock your door daily.

But Priya, he is eight years younger than me.

So what, these days no one cares about age.

Despite being a cardiologist and handsome man too why is he still unmarried? It is doubtful that no girl has proposed to him in this profession.

Leave this aside Vedika, actually these foreigners are very fond of Indian women.

In your family, everyone is busy in their own life; they have no intention to support you emotionally as well financially. Why don't you start a new chapter of your life with this man? You should create your new world and live that life which you have never seen before.

He is asking for my address, wants to send some gift.

So give him your address, what's the problem?

Okay.

Did he ever connect with you on a video call?

Yes twice.

Then it is fine.

Why?

I just asked.

Priya left after two days. For the next five days I was very busy with work. Despite my very busy schedule I was replying his messages. Now I knew his complete routine.

His breakfast is always coffee and bread.

And his favorite Lunch is fish and rice on daily bases.

Sometimes he also eats poga(A dish made with boiled vegetables Sandwiched between the two slice of bread).

He takes his lunch in the hospital and dinner at home prepared by his chef. He doesn't take drinks except red wine.

He owns a penthouse in Great Manchester. He doesn't consume alcohol. On Sundays, he goes to church and then watches a football match in the evening.

He prefers to eat roasted and boiled food instead of fried. He said that in your India, people eat a lot of fried food that is why Indians are very obese and suffering from heart diseases.

Papa, Toady he informed me that he had sent a gift for me which will be delivered by tomorrow.

But I have never asked you for a gift. We should meet once.

No problem darling; will meet very soon.

You haven't seen me yet your complexion is more beautiful than me.

Darling, I have seen you on video call, you are very beautiful.

Don't worry I will give you my color.

I WILL GIVE YOU MY COLOR.

Papa, I was completely mesmerized by his magical words. I didn't know that the heartbeat of love is like this. I used to wait for his call till 2 o'clock every night. I could not sleep unless he talks to me for an hour. For the first time, I realized how sleep vanishes when heart takes over the brain in love.

I still remember Papa, that you used to recite Sant Kabir Das ji's couplet to me -

Love is not cultivated in the garden; love is not sold in the market.

Love always demands one's sacrifice no matter it is king or it is or a common man.

Whoever consumed the nectar of love has surely sacrificed his/her head.

Papa, the next day I got a message from John that the gift parcel has reached Delhi, but you have to pay 300 dollars in order to receive that.

I said but haven't asked any gift from you and if you have already sent it, then why didn't you pay the full amount?

Darling, I have paid for the parcel.

Then why $300?

Darling, I have done the full payment; you have to pay more for the added stuff in the parcel.

No problem, you pay it now, I will return the amount when I come to India.

But I never asked for any gift.

Hey darling, I have sent so many things for you in this parcel.

What have you sent?

Gold anklets, gold earrings, a bracelet, a diamond ring and few pounds in cash.

Why?

Just out of love.

How many pounds?

Not much, just 45000 pounds.

Are you crazy John? Does anyone send money in gift boxes like this?

I do not want any gift nor will I pay any money for that?

Don't you love me?

I don't like to receive gift from a stranger. The customs officials will enquire me.

No darling, I promise they won't enquire about this.

Darling, right now you will get a call from Delhi; you need to transfer $ 300 in Indian currency to the mentioned account.

Listen John very carefully, I will not transfer any money.

Okay darling I am hanging up the phone, I need to rush to the hospital, will call you later.

Looking at my wall clock I assumed, it must be 7 A.M. in Great Manchester, John would be drinking coffee with dry bread. Papa, after listening to his demand of money my brain stopped working and created a conflict between my mind and heart. Today it was half day in school, I reached home very early. At 2.30 I received a call from someone asking. Are you Vedika Singh?

I said yes.

It was a girl speaking in improper English.

May I ask who's calling, please?

I am Alma calling from Delhi; we have received a courier mentioning your name form John Rose. You must pay $ 300 to receive this parcel .As soon as you will pay this will be delivered at your place. I am sending you an Account Number; please deposit the money in it.

Before I could say anything the call got disconnect. But after few seconds there was a message in my inbox mentioning Account Number with detail. I was a little bit surprised to see the account number because it was account of an Indian bank form South India. Then I called Alma, to my surprise this time it was a man's voice. I explained him everything and denied to receive Parcel. He was speaking very good English with a south Indian accent. He handed over the phone to Alma.

I repeated the same statement to her.

Then what should I do with this parcel?

Send it back to Doctor John Rose.

It would cost a very high amount to send these things back because it contains valuable things like Gold, diamond and Many Pounds in cash and also you would have to bear the amount as well as the consequences of returning it back too.

No Problem, take this money from John itself and how do you know there is so much stuff in it?

This was revealed while scanning the parcel.

Papa, I was very scared and I refused to accept the parcel.

John called me at midnight; he asked me in a loving tone, "Darling, why did you refuse the parcel? Only 300 dollars need to be paid.

300 dollars i.e. approximately Rs 21000 Rs/-

Almost.

How do you know about the currency of India?

Darling, there are few patients from India who are undergoing my treatment. That is why I know about the Indian currency. At present one dollar is of Rs 76 so you have to pay only Rs 22800/-. You pay it now and trust me; I will return it back to you.

No John, I don't want any gift, get your parcel back. I am very scared of these customs officials. You should have made full payment while sending the parcel.

Darling, I had paid full.

How Much?

One lac.

Still fell short?

Darling, I didn't have any idea that these people in India would ask for more money?

No problem, I don't want any argument, the matter is over.

Darling, why don't you understand, I have spent a lot of money on this gift. I will have to incur heavy expenses to return it back.

No problem John, spend a little more money and get your parcel back.

I am requesting you to accept this gift.

After hanging up the phone Papa, I blocked that custom office number. But again I got a call from an unknown number. He introduced himself as a custom officer and asked for payment for John's parcel. He told me there was nothing to be afraid of. You make this payment; the parcel will reach your home tomorrow morning. Along with this, we will also issue you a certificate so that you won't face any difficulty in exchanging the currency.

He was speaking very improper English. I asked him to talk in Hindi. He said he does not understand Hindi language and disconnected the call. I was very scared so I blocked that number too.

At midnight John called me, though I was very scared, still I answered his call. Maybe I was in love with him and I slipped in to the thoughts of him that how he filled the void in me which was created by a long period of loneliness. I had never thought that someone would come into my life and knock in such a way that I would never be able to forget him. That face, that voice which was very harsh yet it fascinated me..

He very lovingly asked about my well-being. And said - What did you eat for dinner today?

Darling, are you feeling well?

I am okay.

Darling, why didn't you deposit the money for the parcel?

I got scared John, please get your parcel back.

Why are you afraid, darling? I am always with you?

No John, I don't want any money or gift. Papa, my voice was shaking.

No worries darling, don't get panic, I will get the parcel back.

You know, I also sent you a lot of roses in that parcel.

They must have dried up till now, John, I don't want anything.

Okay darling, I will get the parcel back tomorrow.

Papa, I was very worried about his money, I was worried that somehow his parcel should be returned.

I felt sadness in his voice; he wanted to give me that gift at any cost. May be he had also started loving me. I explained to him that I have everything in my life, just get your parcel back by any means. I am worried about your valuables.

Okay darling, I'll talk to you tomorrow. You know how much I love you; I will not put you in any trouble, saying this he hung up the phone.

Papa, four days have passed, there was no phone call of john. I was very worried about him that he might get into some trouble because of this parcel. I told the whole thing to Priya, she got tense too. I was also anxious for myself that the customs might capture me. I was continuously calling and messaging John, but he did not pick up the phone. After four days, he mentioned that he was keeping busy in hospital in attending several emergency cases. He was working day and night.

Finally he called me on the fifth day.

Darling, I am getting that parcel back, I have spoken to the customs people and you just have to do me a favor.

What is that?

I will give you one of my friend's bank account number of India, you just transfer fifty thousand rupees to this account.

Why do you need fifty thousand?

To offer it to customs officials to retrieve my parcel, If this doesn't go straight you might get in to some difficult situation.

I asked in a terrified tone, can't your friend pay this?

He doesn't have.

Then you send it directly to the customs officials.

Darling, if it was feasible I could have sent it earlier.

Why can't you send?

Due to technical issue I am unable to do any transactions from my bank account. So I'm asking for this help from you.

I asked him to give some time.

Hey darling, what to think about it, it is only about fifty thousand rupees, as soon as you deposit it in my friend's account, he will transfer it to the customs officials. When I will come to India, I give you your money back and also this gift which is only for you.

If I am not able to come to India, I will call you to England. I will marry you in the church, as soon as we get married, you will get citizenship of UK. Then we will be together forever living a very happy married life. You are living alone there too, for what purpose you are staying there?

He said don't think too much and sent his friend's account number. Probably this was an account of a person named as Manoj in state Bank of India in Pune. Now I had his friend's account number. For a long time I kept wondering why John's friend did not have fifty thousand? It created a doubt in me about the honesty of John Rose. My Conscious was not allowing me to send this money. Then a thought struck in my mind if I will not send this money, the impact will be hard on John Rose. Papa, forty-five thousand pounds was a huge amount for me too. Ultimately this fear of my mind compelled me to send the amount.

After three days, John showed me the parcel box with my name and address written on it. He also showed ornaments, Pounds and withered rose flowers which he had sent for me which washed my all doubts. It took me by surprise to know that the parcel reached to him so quickly. Not bothering too much on my second thought, I took a sigh of relief that the problem is resolved.

It became a routine for us to chat via messages and voice calls. I was completely immersed in colors of his love. Papa, you used to say that love and peace are two strong pillars which can behold us throughout our life regardless of any difficulties and struggles, Love is the only element which everyone is longing for in his or her life. One day John mentioned that he is planning to construct a hospital in Turkey.

Turkey? Why not In England? I have earned a huge amount of money, and I want to invest this money to build a hospital in Turkey. After that I will designate an eligible person to run that hospital and will travel the whole world with you.

But why in Turkey?

Darling, don't you like Turkey?

No, I just asked. Okay darling, now I have to pack my luggage. Tomorrow morning I have a flight to Turkey, i will call you once I reach there. Papa, I have many confusions and doubts in my mind to share with you. But I am exhausted now and I will surely tell in next letter, it is 12 o'clock at night.

Rest in next letter

With love

Your daughter vedika

Papa, please wait.

******

Third letter

(Turkey and that corridor of a five-star hotel)

My Dear Papa

How are you?

You must have received my earlier letters and you are aware about the situation till now. This letter will also surprise you? Your reading and writing speed is very high. I know that you are very curious to know everything about your daughter. Did she get the seven colors of the rainbow in her life that she always yearned?

I am already late to write this letter so I am quickly coming on the main topic without any preamble.

It was the very cool morning of 5th December 2021. You must remember how cold is used to in Lucknow, specifically in the months of December and January. Anyway, this was one of your favorite cities. The language used to so polite that a sweet flow of speech was found in this city due to the confluence of Urdu, Persian and Hindi. But now everyone's language is spoiled. Slangs are in trend now English language is a must to have an impactful personality.

John messaged me, that he had reached Turkey safely and his hospital work had started. He was staying in a five star hotel and he was keeping busy with his work. Now he was able to talk in morning and evening only due to time difference. One day he asked my date of birth. I requested him not to send any parcel again.

Oh so you are also born on 21st December, I was also born on this date. It is great that we will celebrate our birthday together.

I am going to Great Manchester from Turkey on 19th December and my brother Joel will also join me. We both have a planned to celebrate birthday as well as Christmas with our parents in Italy.

While you are in Italy who will look after the work of your hospital?

Darling, I will come back to Turkey on 2nd January.

How many days leave have you applied for?

One and a quarter month.

Do they allow you to take leave for so long period?

Yes darling, I have earned lot of respect in my hospital. This project in Turkey will take almost six months to Complete. Once I am done with this project I will send you sponsorship paper required for VISA to come to England.

No, I don't wish to come to England, I like my Country only.

Darling, if you wish I will come along with you to India. I can also build a hospital there too.

Do you have that much money, John?

Yes darling, I have.

Following these words I felt, my days were flying with the wind, as if every day had a new wing. I was flying in a sky that I had never even imagined. A sky chirping with birds, a sky full of flowers fragrances

Priya often used to ask about him on phone.

On December 10, 2021, John told me that he had left with no cash and his master card was also not working.

No problem, you must have entered wrong pin number several time so they have blocked your card. You please connect with their customer care number and request to resolve this problem.

I already did that darling.

So what did they say?

They said that it will take forty-eight hours to reactivate your card.

Then I think you won't face any problem in this hotel at least they will provide meals.

That is okay but I have not eaten anything since three days.

But I was surprised to know about this because every five star hotel charges for room always include breakfast.

This is not the case for this hotel, I have done payments only for accommodation: I have been eating meals from outside till now. I had no money so I could not visit my hospital site too.

So for how many days has your card been blocked?

It's been three days darling.

So is it not activated yet?

Despite requesting several time the bank has not resolved this issue.

John, usually bank responses prompt after saying this I started thinking that the poor guy has been hungry for three days.

Papa, I tried to convince him a lot that he should talk to the bank people again. Hearing my arguments he became irritated and said that I am dying of hunger here and you are preaching to me. If you can do something, please help me.

How can I help you from here?

You send me twelve thousand rupees according to your Indian currency. This money would be sufficient for two days meal.

Two days' food for twelve thousand, I was stunned?

Yes darling, food here is very expensive.

But how will I send you money?

Your bank account is in England, anyway your ATM card is not working and how can I send you money abroad? This is not possible John.

An Employee of this hotel named Delia has family in India, so you can transfer the amount to his wife's account. As soon as you wiil transfer, I will get the money here from Delia in cash.

John, can't you borrow the money from Delia?

He will not agree to this.

Why, you both are Christian; is he not supposed to help you?

He has already refused that's why I am asking you .And he has agreed on twenty percent commission to receive this money. I am dying of hunger here and you are preaching again.

Ok, you send me the account number.

John sent the account number; it was the account of State Bank of India Of Bangalore city. The account holder lady had a strange name - Velma Kasokar. John received money; I took a sigh of relief that today he ate food after three days. John's Master Card was not fixed; he told that his card would be fixed only after reaching England. I kept depositing money to Delia's account on every second day till 18th December 2021 in name of hunger. John's flight ticket was booked for 19th December. On 20th December 2021, he along with his brother reached his parents' place in Italy.

His birthday was on 21st December 2021 and so was mine. Papa, he wished me on that day and also made me talk to his parents on video call. Joel also talked to me, I was very happy. His parents told me that now you are a member of our family, soon we are willing you to marry John, do you agree? Papa, despite having doubts about john and his family, i nodded my head in yes doubting that they could also be involved in human trafficking and that could be dangerous for me too.

I felt a momentary Xenophobia, yet I was very happy which I cannot describe in words. You can imagine the extent of my happiness, Papa. There is no need for me to tell you or explain. You understood my silence very well whether it was of sadness or happiness.

John returned on 7th January 2022 to Great Manchester. He said that his bank account issue has been resolved. This time while travelling to, Turkey he is carrying twenty thousand dollar cash with him. He reached Turkey and got busy with his hospital work. He wanted to complete this work fast so that he can travel the whole world with me. *(Repetition of this statement influenced my heart and my mind too)* Papa, I was also roaming in the world of dreams with him and was creating an imaginary and beautiful world for us.

I even asked him with surprise, can you take this much cash with you? Won't this be objectionable by airport authority?

No darling, there is no restriction on carrying cash anywhere in our country?

Every time I used to repeat same question, why are you building a hospital in Turkey and not somewhere else?

His answer was always the same that if you wish we can build at any other place too.

I assumed that he is a religious person because he never missed praying in church on Sundays.

One day John told that the cash he had brought with him had been stolen.

I got a shock and asked how?

I kept in my hotel room; perhaps the room service guy had stolen them.

So why did you not complain to the hotel official?

You could have carried it with you?

It was risky to carry the cash at the hospital site.

What are the hotel people saying?

I spoke to the hotel manager but they are denying it.

This is really bad. Which type of five star hotels is this?

Papa, I felt very sorry for him and consoled him saying that don't get panic, you do have an ATM card.

No darling, my master card has been blocked again.

Why is it blocked? You recently got it rectified by the bank?

Again I entered the wrong PIN several times.

Oh, then you do one thing, go back to Great Manchester, get your card sorted there and then come back. And why do you enter wrong PIN again, every time your card gets blocked.

Darling, I can't go back to Great Manchester now.

Why?

My return ticket is of 27th February 2022.

Oh, then reschedule your ticket.

I am trying to convey this neither I have money nor the card to pay the dues charged by the hotel.

So you had not deposited the hotel money yet?

I have deposited the advanced and rest I was supposed to pay at check out time.

Can't you request a favor from hotel authority to book your ticket or they can connect with your hospital of Great Manchester to acknowledge your identity.

I tried hard but they are not cooperating.

I became very upset after hearing all this.

Do one thing darling?

I asked hesitantly what can I do for you?

Please send some money in Delia's Account.

How Much John?

Rs 20000/- in your currency. As soon as I reach Great Manchester I will return your money including the earlier amount too.

I transferred Rs 20,000 to Delia's account.

Papa, after that John gave me many account numbers, all of them were of Indian government banks. I kept sending them Rs 20,000 on alternate day. One day I asked John - how do you collect this money?

Darling, the accounts I have sent you all work in Turkey but their families live in India, Delia knows them very well. And Delia charges Rs 2000 as commission on Rs 10000.

Impermissible brokerage! One can stoop so low for money. Delia is taking advantage of John's terrible and helpless situation and minting money out of sin. There should be always being trust relationship between the member of same communities staying in unfamiliar country which John and Delia both were lacking.

John, how many days will be taken to complete this hospital work? How are you managing your visit to the hospital and expenses there? Is food that expensive abroad?

With the money you are sending, I eat food one day and remain hungry the other day because I also have to pay the taxi fare from it. A lot of work is still pending.

John, do you still go to church?

Yes darling I do.

John, the day after tomorrow is Sunday, this time you tell your entire problem to the pastor, he will definitely help you.

Oh darling, I didn't even think of this. You are so intelligent and beautiful too, that's why I love you so much. I will go tomorrow, surely discuss my problem hoping for the help.

John went to church on Sunday but he didn't receive any help from church.

A second thought flashed in my mind that Christians had converted many Hindus and Muslims of India to their religion by providing monthly living allowance from church and securing jobs in private sectors especially in the missionary schools. One of my friend's husband suddenly changed his religion and threw away all the idols from his house. Despite being a staunch sanatani and economically sound he adopted Christianity raises a strong question that how are they forcibly indoctrinate people. Earlier he used to recite RAMAYAN a divine sacred scripture of Hindu Religion now he has become a daily visitor of church.

Why their ideology overturned upside down in John's case. Papa, I said all this to John and he replied that Turkey is a Muslim majority Country which includes only 2 percent of our community. Due to scarcity of funds, church authority is unable to help me. The work of his hospital was continuing because he had already paid advance to the contractor.

I used to feel very sad that he eats one day and remains hungry the next day. A few days were left for 27th February; all his problems would be over once he will return to Great Manchester.

Suddenly a news flashed on television about the commencement unceasing war between Russia and Ukraine on 24th February 2022, due to which from 26th Feb

2022, Turkey suspended all airport services for indeterminate time.

As a result of this Johns trouble escalated further, the hotel manager shifted his luggage from the room to Hotels corridor.I was shocked after knowing this how can someone behave so inhumanly? I was also running out of money. Gradually my bank account became almost empty as well as prya's account also. After few days Turkey resumed its airport services. John's ticket for 27th February was reinstated but he did not have money for the taxi so he could not reach the airport and his ticket also became null.

Now neither Priya nor I were able to help him so I requested him to ask help from his family.

He said Papa can't help.

You said that you have a rich back ground then why can't your father help you in this horrifying situation? Can't he transferred the money to Delia's account?

No, he can't.

Why John?

He is an elderly person and won't be able to handle the bank work.

There is no need to go to the bank, everything is online and he can easily transfer the amount sitting at home.

Darling, first of all they don't know how to transfer online and I haven't told them anything about my situation yet. He will get upset and won't be able to bear it, might be he dies and I don't want to lose my father.

I also got worried after hearing this.

John called at night. He was moaning. I asked John where you are?

Darling,in the corridor of the hotel.

But how can a hotelier do this?

Is there no one in hotel who can help you? I think other Guests must be staying there too. Can't you request to them to help you?

No darling, I asked everyone but no one is willing to help me.

I was also spending sleepless night thinking about John sleeping in the corridor of the hotel.

Then I asked him at night, is there nobody to help you in your family and friends?

I can't ask from family or friends because they will reveal my situation to my father.

So doesn't your father know that you are in Turkey?

No darling, I told them I was in Turkey on work but had returned to Great Manchester before the war started.

Papa, John was hungry. It had been four days since he had eaten. I took a loan of Rs 2 lakhs on my credit card from the bank for him. Again the sequence of sending money started but it didn't suffice for many days. Considering his condition I suggested him to ask for at least one meal from church.

Somehow he managed to contact a poor helper at church who came to Turkey on 15 days leave from some other country.

I kept wondering what I could do to get John back from Turkey to Great Manchester. Whenever I ask John where are you?

I am sitting in the corridor darling. The church man has gone back to his duty. Now no one is going to feed me here. I am very hungry Darling; I will die out of hunger right here in this corridor. This hotel corridor will become a grave for me.

He told that he is not able to sleep at night because of cold weather and mosquitoes in the corridor. My Condition is dreadful here now, darling do something for me.

I could imagine how helpless is john lying in the corridor of the hotel.

I thought of all possible ways to help him and finally landed up taking one more loan of Rs 2 Lakhs from bank. But that too worked for few days only. Again due to short of money he remained hungry for next three days. He used to cry a lot, Papa; I too had tears in my eyes. Whenever I asked John, where are you? In a very low voice he would tell me that he was in the corridor.

Now I started hating this corridor, I did not have left money for my daily basic expenses; there was no question for sending him. I was unable to focus my work. My mind was busy in finding all possibilities for arranging money for him so that he can fly back to Great Manchester as early as possible.

Suddenly I thought of his brother Joel staying in Scotland why can't he help john. John told that Joel had an accident and he has been in the hospital since a month. He had severe injuries on face and jaw due to which doctor has advised him to stay quiet.

Does your father know about Joel's accident?

No, it can him impact badly.

We did not tell them anything. I used to listen to John's voice amid the noise of the corridor along with people foot step sound and closing and opening of hotel rooms too. There was restricted wi fi in corridor so video calls were not possible .I could feel the pain and need of food in his dull and moaning voice. But only one question was prevailing on my mind how will john get rid of this wretched corridor? It seemed as if this corridor had become John's life and mine too. Will he ever be able to come out of this corridor?

I called joel to explain john's condition but a strange person received the call and introduced himself as Joel's friend named Kelvin.

Can I speak to Joel?

No he can't talk right now.

Doctor has advised him to take three days rest so he will be able to talk after that.

Okay then do a video call Kelvin, I wanted to see him.

No, video call is not allowed in the Hospital.

Are you aware of John's situation he had stuck in corridor of hotel in Turkey, and he didn't even have money for food.

Yes I know everything Vedia?

Vediya, who is this Vediya?

John has told that your name is Vedia, you are helping him a lot.

I became silent on hearing this; John had once called me by this name. I laughed a lot, Papa, but he could not pronounce my name properly. After giving up, he said, Darling, I like call you Darling only.

Joel's condition became more serious so Kelvin could not reach him. Somehow I sent 8000 rupees to John so that he could eat food. His voice seemed as if he was taking his last breath.

I don't know after how many days t John had eaten food but this money was sufficient only for one day. Three days passed again, John was sitting hungry in the corridor of the hotel which was probably going to become his grave after few days. I was praying to God day and night that somehow he should return to his hospital in Great Manchester.

I again told John to connect with his hospital authority to help him.

They are not helping me but today they have sent me an email that if I do not join my duty within a week then they will terminate me.

Oh, so you tell them your problem. He will definitely help you.

John asks for 15 days time from them; write an email to the hospital requesting them to grant you Fifteen days time. At least your job will be safe. By then Kelvin will also reach you.

Papa, he did whatever I said.

I also spoke to Joel, he was barely able to speak, he told me that Kelvin would be reaching John the day after tomorrow and then he would be going to Great Manchester. After a few days he will come to Scotland to meet me, now I will never let him go to Turkey.

Then how john will manage to complete his hospital work?

We will sell it, that place is not favorable for us.

Yes, I had told this too John.

Joel, have you informed John that Kelvin will reach him day after tomorrow?

No darling, I called but he did not pick up, now I am worried about John. You convey to him that Kelvin will reach Turkey day after tomorrow with 10,000 dollars.

Similarities in their voices always keep on confusing me Papa.

I don't know why for the first time I had some doubt, I asked him whether he was John or Joel.

Darling I am Joel, what's wrong with you? You are calling on my number.

So why are you calling me darling?

Oh darling, we call everyone darling here.

Even Dogs and cats too.

Oh, he laughed and then said yes darling.

I could not send money to john; he has not contacted me for three days. Then I called Joel but his phone was also switched off, perhaps he has still not recovered fully. On the fourth day, John called at midnight, I almost cried and asked him - John, how are you, why haven't you called for so many days, did Kelvin reach to you or not?

There was silence for a moment, then a voice came - I am Kelvin, I have just reached Turkey. I've come to take John with me; Joel has sent ten thousand dollars for him. I have booked tickets for tomorrow but I could not find John in the Hotel.

I was shocked to hear that voice, this time I strongly believed that it was john's voice.

Are you kidding me, Kelvin probably reached you that's why you are happy.

No, I am Kelvin.

Why do your voice resemble to twin brothers? And how do you know that you have to call only me?

I saw your several messages in his phone and he has saved your number as "my wife" that is why I called you first, knowing that you will be worried about him.

What nonsense are you talking, you are John, why are you kidding me, please stop it?

Don't bother me,

But papa, he was Kelvin, he shouted angrily at me I am not finding John here and you are troubling me.

Please enquire about him from the hotel staff?

They have kept his luggage in the corridor.

Then where is John, Kelvin?

Let me ask from the Hotel Staff please.

You asked Delia, he will surely know about john.

A few minutes later, Kelvin told that looking at his health, the hotel authority has admitted him to the hospital. I got entangled in queries raised in my mind thinking that if the hotel staff could not feed him then how could they send him to hospital without charging any money?

Saying this that john has not eaten food for many days, Just rush to the hospital immediately. I was surprised and almost screamed when he said that t he is tired and will go to see him tomorrow Morning. After saying this he disconnected and switched off the phone.

The next day John called at 10 am. I couldn't recognize the voice again. I said very angrily, Kelvin, did you have enough sleep? Shame on you, how mean are you don't you have any feeling? Before I could say something else I heard a faint voice saying darling I am John.

How are you John? Where's Kelvin? He is a very selfish man.

How is your health now, what happened that you had to come to the hospital?

Due to hunger, my organs stopped working and I became unconscious. Then the hotel people threw me here.

Oh, these people are so insensitive?

And where is your luggage John?

Darling in the corridor, the hotel staff has also confiscated my passport.

Oh so how will you go without a passport?

They will hand over my passport only after settling the hotel dues.

Please make me talk to Kelvin.

He has gone to get food for me.

Did he give the money to you which joel has sent for you?

Not now, I am very weak so he will get the ticket rescheduled for tomorrow.

Papa, that day, we talked several time but Kelvin was not there.

When Kelvin didn't return till late evening I said to John to call him.

I have already called him several times but his phone is switched off.

Why didn't you call Joel?

I called Joel; the doctor told that he can't talk right now.

Why, he talked to me that day.

His health has deteriorated again, he is unconscious. John started crying while saying this.

You give me Kelvin's number.

Darling, he has run away with the money. There is no use; he will not answer the phone.

What do you mean by this?

But he is Joel's friend. How could he do that, John?

Please give me his number.

I dialed Kelvin's number several times but in vain. Holding my head, I was forced to think about the man who had come here specifically to help John. Why did he run away?

How to help John now my brain stooped working. I had no money left and couldn't figure out what to do.

John, when will you get discharged from the hospital?

When all payments and formalities will be completed.

You could have mentioned about you to these people, they will surely consider your problem on behalf of having same profession.

Despite mentioning about my profession they are not ready to cooperate with me. May be I do not belong their community.

So what is the meaning of taking the doctors' Hippocratic Oath?

Darling I don't understand.

Doctors take the Hippocratic Oath during their studies, have you forgotten?

Oh yes darling, who believes these things now a days, no one keeps the oath.

(Note: The Hippocratic Oath is an oath historically taken by physicians and other medical professionals. It was written by Hippocrates - its essence is that a physician will treat a patient for his or her benefit keeping his or her secrets confidential and A physician will never take any profit or money for treatment from another physician. There are many other things included in this oath but this is enough here. Hippocrates was the father of modern medicine.)

Why does Dr. John not know about the Hippocratic Oath, I thought for a while but once again my heart won and my mind remained far behind, as if it got lost somewhere?

Suddenly I thought of Delia that he can help you to get your hospital documents.

Which hospital's papers darling?

Hey, the same which you are building in Turkey.

Yes, but we are two partners in this hospital.

But you did not mention this before?

No, I did but you probably forgot.

Come on, Instead of asking help from your partner you are lying down just like an idiot in this corridor? You take money from your partner and go away from here.

My partner has refused to provide any help.

Oh then the other only option left is to sell your share.

Okay, that I can try for.

After two days, John got discharged from hospital and thanked me many times. I was feeling proud of dealing with this problem with great finesse.

He told that he will book the ticket tomorrow.

The next day I called to find out for what date his ticket is booked. He told that he could not book the ticket.

Why? You have money with you.

No I am left with no money.

What do you mean by this?

The hotel charges are not cleared yet. The money which I got in exchange for hospital document is adjusted with my treatment and medicine. They did not return my passport.

Papa, I was very surprised to know that despite having so much money, the hotel outstanding amount is still not paid! Ignoring my second thought I asked him-

Where are you now John?

This time his answer poked me deep inside that I am in the corridor.

Oh no, again same corridor?

Did Joel contact you?

No Darling.

And what about Kelvin?

I know nothing about him.

What will you do now, John? Is there no one at your Great Manchester hospital who can help you with this problem?

No darling.

There must be someone from your staff or colleague.

Yes, there is a nurse who works in my hospital; she is ready to help me on her condition.

What is that?

She is saying, she can take me out of here but before that she will send a contract letter.

That means any agreement?

Yes.

What is that agreement about?

The agreement puts a condition to marry her.

So John, what is the problem in accepting that.

You are crazy darling, how can I marry someone else when I only love you?

Hey John, first come out of this situation by any mean then do whatever you want.

This can't happen; women have a lot of rights in our England. If I divorce her after marrying, I will have to give my entire property.

So what is the problem in doing this?

No darling, instead of doing this I will prefer to die in this corridor.

Did she send you the contract letter?

Yes darling, she has sent it on What's app.

So John, please go ahead.

But papa, he did not sign that letter.

Papa, again the same question raised in front of me that how to save John from this horrifying situation. After searching on Google I found about the bus service from Turkey to The Great Manchester charging a fare of 8000 Rupees Only. I told John to leave his luggage in hotel and fetch the next Bus from Bus Terminal. I am borrowing 20000 rupees from a friend and I will transfer that to Delia's account tomorrow. You can Plan to collect your documents and passport form the hotel in your next visit.

The next day John booked the bus ticket, he told me that the Bus from Turkey to Great Manchester ply twice a week.

I have bought a ticket for Wednesday and saved the money for the taxi, and food too. To save this money I have to skip tomorrow's meal and he cried a lot after saying this. I too had tears in my eyes but there was a feeling of peace that now he will reach his penthouse in Great Manchester and he will be able to relish his favorite dishes prepared by his chef. Finally after facing this difficult time he will meet his own people and will have sound sleep in his bed.

And his own breaths too.

On Wednesday morning John called me and said that he would leave the hotel quiet early to avoid risk of missing although the bus time was in evening. And don't worry; I will call you once I reach Great Manchester.

When I didn't receive any call next day I got worried about him. Then I called him to ask where he is now?

John said crying, in the corridor.

In which corridor?

In the corridor of the same hotel.

But why, I almost screamed.

Actually, I was supposed to pay the insurance money also along with the ticket.

What does insurance money mean?

Who takes the insurance money for the bus travel?

No darling, they charge here.

So why didn't you give it?

I didn't know this when I booked the ticket and yesterday I didn't have money left with me. Now they have rescheduled my ticket for Friday.

So now how much money you require?

Just send 20000 more, I will have food here for two days and I will reach home on Saturday morning.

John, are you out of your mind, you know how much money I have transferred for this. I already have a huge debt of bank on my head and also borrowed money on Five percent interest from one of my friend. Saying this I cried loudly. I felt like I have gone crazy. Hearing my cry, John also cried a lot and said – Darling, please stop crying I will stay in this corridor till Joel Comes to take me .**Darling now I love this corridor**.

Saying this he stared laughing to hide his pain which I could feel very clearly.

With great difficulty I transferred Rs. 20000/- to Delia's account. I was very anxious thinking that he had not eaten for two days and lying again in the same corridor.

I did not know that I would never be able to forget the pain given by this Corridor.

On Friday morning John called me after reaching the bus stand and said I will call you after reaching Great Manchester, Now don't worry and Sleep peacefully. I felt an uncertain fear in his shivering voice. He had not eaten food for two days. My soul was crying.

I could not sleep the whole night, kept praying to God that there should be no hindrance of any kind.

At night while I was repeatedly checking my mobile I saw message on my Face book account. He was a doctor named George Paul, who was asking for my phone number. I ignored that message.

It was my holiday on Saturday, at 2 'O clock John called to inform that he had reached home safely in Great Manchester, he cried a lot and thanked me saying this that he will eat properly and never sleep in a corridor again. Tomorrow I will go to church and the day after tomorrow to my hospital. Then I'll go to see Joel. I am coming to India soon to meet you. Your money also has to be paid. You have helped me a lot.

it was the month of July when he returned to his home after 7 months. It was a relaxing and relieving moment for me after a long time. I never told John that I too had not eaten food when he was hungry.

The Papa, I was very afraid that John might become a corridor man like the terminal man.

War between Russia and Ukraine was still continuing.

Papa Terminal Man is the story of a refugee who lived at the airport terminal for 18 years.

There are many people in this world who are homeless. But how will a person who does not belong to any country can survive in this world? This is the story of Mehran Kareemi from Iran; he went to England in 1973 to pursue his graduation course. There was an Islamic revolution going on in Iran at that time, Mehran Kareemi also took part in that movement. Because he was a revolutionary, so the Iranian government ordered his deportation. The royal family of Iran also cancelled his citizenship. Mehran Kareemi now became a refugee. The UN of Belgium provided him a refugee certificate so that he could live in any European country. On 26th 1988, he left for London from France but his briefcase was stolen along with all his papers. As a result British airport deported him back to Paris.

At Paris he was arrested because of lack of documents needed. He was not allowed to go out of the airport. He requested to the Belgian authorities to issue him a refugee certificate again. But that did not work out. He was given permission to stay at the departure lounge of Terminal Number One in Paris. As the time passed by, Terminal One became his home; he was offered food from the airport lounge authority. A French lawyer fought for him but in vain. He studied economics while staying at this airport. In 2003, veteran Hollywood director Steven Spielberg made a film named "The Terminal" on his life and bought the copyrights of his life and gave him a cheque of two and a half million dollars in return. But Kareemi did not have any bank account to accept this amount because he was not having any authorized citizenship of any country. 18 years passed and he got a house through the help and efforts made by the Red Cross Authority. Mehran Kareemi died on 12th November 2022. He is also known as Alfred Kareemi. He wrote his own autobiography on which Berg made a film.

And this film became a huge hit and earned in crores. What a tragedy it was that the person on whom life this film was made he had neither a house nor citizenship of any country. Perhaps this is such a unique case in the world which is both, the first and the last. The Heart wrenching story tells us how this man sitting at the terminal one of Lounge of Paris Airport became a sufferer and an observer who witnessed all facets of his life and arduous journey from living luxurious life style to horrendous incidences which landed him empty handed at the end.

A promising son, a promising person but everything was lost .Many human rights organizations also made a lot of efforts for him, but every effort became null in front of fate and cruel and insensitive law made by this cruel world.

I was also afraid that John Rose might also become Mehran Kareemi.

Papa Take care of yourself

Rest in Next

Vedika

******

Fourth Letter

(The Imposter)

Papa

John went to see Joel and returned to his duties at his hospital in Great Manchester. He asked that how much money I owe you.

Eighteen Lakh.

Okay Darling Please sends me your bank account number so that I will transfer this money to your account. I asked him whether technical issue of his bank account is resolved .He Said it is fixed now I can transfer money to your account. Now every problem is over. Would it be safe to transfer such a big amount without any problem?

Absolutely fine and safe darling, because this is account to account transfer. And I am coming to India to meet you on 12th September 2022.

I sent him my bank account number. He shared the photo of his ticket. This was a ticket from Great Manchester to Mumbai.

I asked why Mumbai?

Darling, I have an hour's work in Mumbai, my flight will land at Mumbai airport by 10 A.M. and I will reach in Lucknow by evening. Even from Delhi I will have to come to Lucknow.

They have granted me fifteen days leave to visit India.

Fifteen days? What will you do here for so long?

He laughed too loudly saying, "What else, I will travel India with you?"

You are so innocent darling I am only coming to meet you.

And have you booked a hotel to stay?

Why hotel darling? I will stay with you.

With me! No Point at all.

Darling, is there any problem in staying with you?

No, we don't allow strangers in our house.

But I am not a stranger any more.

Look John, you are neither my relative nor my spouse yet. So I cannot stay with you this is our Indian tradition.

So I am coming to marry you. Tomorrow I will transfer money to your account.

Next day John told that he has deposited 48 lakhs cash in my account.

Why 48 lakhs, you have to give only 18 lakhs.

I am sending this extra money in advance to utilize during my stay in India.

So why did you deposit the cash instead of account to account transfer.

Again due to some Technical issue account to account transfer was not feasible so I deposited cash in your account. Soon you will receive a mail asking about mandatory detail about you. Once you will send all the required detail the money will be transferred to your account. Darling, I am going to the hospital now, will talk to you in the evening.

Papa, Rs 48 lakhs is getting transferred to my account from abroad so i got scared. I refused to accept money from him and I suggested that he could give the money physically, during his visit to India.

Hey darling, why are you so nervous? I am here for you I am very busy, let's talk in the evening and yes, remember to scan all your documents and send them in the mail. Only then will the money come to your account.

John tried to convince a lot to me but still I was scared. It seemed as if a huge storm was about to come. I was going through a tremendous pressure as if a goods train is passing through an old age bridge which does not have the capacity to hold it any more. Papa, this train was crushing my heart for many months, probably ever since John Rose came into my life. I was sitting in the staff room of the school when a teacher came there and seeing me she asked - What happened to you Vedika? Why has your face turned so pale? I said nothing and went straight to bank from school.

On enquiring the bank manager told if the person who is depositing the amount is in your blood relation then there will be no problem?

Does this require submission of my personal detail to sender's bank?

No, just account number, branch and IFSC code is enough.

The bank manager asked whether this amount is bank transfer only.

I said no.

Then?

It is cash.

How much cash?

About 48 lakhs.

No madam, this might put you in deep trouble. Reserve Bank of India and Income Tax Department will enquire for clearing documents from you.

But he has already deposited the money in my account.

No problem, our bank will send a mail to you asking for your permission to accept or deny this amount.

You don't accept it, there is nothing to fear. By the way, may I know who is sending you money so foolishly?

I have a doctor friend in England.

Despite being educated, he is doing this stupidity?

Do you know him?

Yes, very well.

Then it's okay.

I asked you all this because several frauds are happening these days.

What kind of fraud?

Some people deposit their cash which is black money in someone's account to convert it to white. Too many foreigners are committing these frauds to take undue advantage of Indians.

These people have accounts here in India also, like first they will deposit cash in your account and then they will get it transferred to their account and will give you some commission. A person gets badly trapped in the greed of this commission.

I came home from school and saw that there was a mail from Vista Limited Company. They mentioned that Dr. John Rose has deposited 48 lakhs in your account, for which we need a scanned copy of your Aadhar Card, PAN Card and Driving License.

I immediately replied to them that I do not want this money. Return this money to John.

Immediately they send a mail mentioning that the money can't be returned once it has been deducted from sender's account.

Sorry I will not accept this money, I replied them.

After that there were several mails from that company but i ignored all. At night John called me. He was very angry that earlier also you had done this, you did not take my gift and now you are not even taking the money. You are an idiot, does anyone refuse for money?

But John you are supposed to send only eighteen lakhs.

John said first you refused to accept the gift and now the money. Now I will give you your money only after coming to India.

No need to shout at me it was your fault to deposit cash.

Again a technical issue happened with my account that is why I did it. Now i lost huge amount only because of you.

Why won't you get it back?

I will explain everything to you personally once I reached to India on 12th September.

Papa, I talked to John that day but I was having an apprehension in me. If the money would have come to the bank, I would probably have been trapped.

Many times many thoughts would come to my mind but I shook them off.

But Papa, One issue was troubling me most that after reaching India, he will stay at my place which I never wanted.

Suddenly Many Doctors sent request on my Face book and Insta gram account, it was really surprising for me but I didn't pay any attention to them at that moment.

It was 12th September 2022 morning, the day for which I was eagerly waiting. I received a phone call from John Rose mentioning that he has arrived at Mumbai Airport.

I burst with joy, John, have you reached Mumbai?

Saying yes darling, he also laughed.

So you will reach Lucknow by evening, tell me what time you will reach, I will come to pick you up.

But darling, there's a problem. Mumbai Airport Authority has stopped me and these people are interrogating me a lot.

Why did they stop you, I was very surprised. Have you carried any suspicious stuff or unaccounted money with you?

No darling, they are just inquiring.

Who are they who is interrogating?

An officer from the immigration department.

What are they asking?

They are asking for the purposes have I come here.

So why didn't you inform them?

I have told that I have come here to meet my wife.

I was shocked and said have you gone crazy, I am not your wife.

So what, now that I am here to marry you. The officer will call you; I have given him your phone number.

After some time, I got a call from immigration department of Mumbai Airport Authority asking, "Are you Vedika?

Papa, I was very nervous and afraid of this unanticipated inquiry.

It seemed a very familiar Man's voice to me speaking in improper English. Before i could recognize that person he said do you know Doctor John Rose who has come from Great Manchester?

Yes, I know him; he is my very good friend.

What's the matter officer - I asked fearfully.

Nothing, his papers are incomplete, so we have stopped him here at the airport.

What will he have to do for that?

He will have to deposit Rs 80,000/- .

Let me speak to him.

I told John that you have brought money with you, deposit Rs 80,000/-

I have not brought money; I have an ATM card which is not working here.

So how will you tackle this problem because I don't have any money to send you?

Please arrange this amount by anyways or else they will put me in jail.

John was pleading badly. I said, give me some time, I will see if any arrangement is possible, what will they do if money is not deposited ?

Nothing darling, they will send me back.

While thinking of any possibility to arrange this money, I started scrolling his pictures saved in my Phone Gallery. Suddenly in one of his photos, I saw him sitting on a doctor's' chair with a different name plate which Jerked my mind. I zoomed that photo to see it clearly. The name written on the plate was Doctor Benton Naskun.

The effort to identify the suspicious voice of the officer prevailed on my mind and I focused on of this strong substantial Pointer. Earlier too, I raised the same question in front of John after seeing this photo. He told that at that time he was sitting on the seat of another doctor named as Benton Naskun.

The dense Perplexity of brain forced me to search that name on Google. Finally the mystery of imposter John Rose unfolded in front of me knowing that Doctor Benton Naskun and Ben Naskun were gynecologists specialized in test tube babies IVF procedure and running their own private Clinic in Turkey. In This confused state I gave that number to Priya asking her to enquire and know the validity of number. After a short while, Priya informed me that number belongs to a courier office near the airport in Bangalore. I couldn't believe it. While I was talking to priya again I received a call from same number.

This time I recognized that suspicious voice, it was same person who called up for the gift in the very beginning.

I said yes in heated voice.

Madam, are you sending 80000/- Rs for John Rose?

I said very calmly No Sir.

Then we will put him in jail.

Yes please I will be happy.

That officer kept silent. I remained sitting like a statue; it seemed as if the breath had gone out of my body. Such a big betrayal, such a deceit. Heart was deceived in this way, just to rob the money, saying that he was lying hungry in the corridor of a hotel. How can somebody play with someone's feelings like this, my heart was deeply hurt. A stream of tears flowed from the eyes. There was a storm in my mind with anger; I had never thought that this corridor would give me such a flood in which everything of mine would be swept away. There will be a stench of memories left behind which will always haunt me. It is said that even the deepest wound heals with time, but this was a canker sore, how will it heal?

I was sitting there, bewildered, as if someone had snatched away everything from me, money can be earned again but scar made by this incident will never fade away. I was in love with that face, that broken voice was the heartbeat of my heart. It seemed as if I would fall right now. Lava blazed in my heart and I wept bitterly. I felt like screaming so loud that my scream should tear the sky apart. Today I wanted to shake the entire universe. Papa, was I so stupid? What was my fault? Just that I loved that unknown face? Saying this I started weeping again. Who was listening to my pain here, father? These walls of the room or this mobile in my hand which became the tool to ruin my life.

My phone was ringing continuously; it was John Rose's phone. I kept looking at that phone for a long time, for the first time I felt that this is not a phone but an atom bomb, as soon as I hold it in my hand it will explode and blow me in to several pieces and these walls will burst, everything will be destroyed, no one will be able to find even the ashes of my existence. One phone call and life is over. Just one word darling, and the whole existence merges into it?

I picked up the phone while sobbing; John asked in a very nervous voice - What happened darling, why are you crying? The moment he could say anything else I screamed -

You impersonator, stop this drama now.

What do you mean darling, why are you saying like that? I'm your John Rose, your own John Rose. And why did you tell the officer to put me in jail?

Because you are an impersonator, you have used the face of Dr. Naskun; he is a gynecologist doctor in Turkey, not in London. They are twin brothers and he is running his own private clinic.

No darling, you have some misunderstanding.

Will you stop professing now?

Papa, at first he kept trying to make me believe that I had become a victim of some misunderstanding.

At last he admitted that he had deceived and robbed me by using Dr Naskun's face.

I want to see your actual face john.

I will tell you the whole story why I did this? But now the truth is that I have started loving you very much while robbing you. Just help me this time. I only want $ 500, not more.

Now I realize that I was talking and expressing my feeling in front of a façade character masked behind a beautiful face.

I said I am giving your number to the police.

He replied very comfortably, first of all, you cannot do this because you have fallen in love with Naskun's face. That means you love me.

The second thing is that no police can catch us. You will never file a complaint against me to save your esteemed respect.

Respect?

This is what he said that because of your respect you will not go to the police.

I kept wondering whether it is the fear of respect or emotions that stops us.

In reality, people do not dare to file the complaint against these crimes. First of all police always put you in a questionable position by assuming you a stupid person and ignoring emotions at all .The world has become a play Ground of money and material creating a huge void and desolation within one's life impacting our society. in such a hard time when our own people don't support and stand with us then how can one expect any supportive action from this rigid police department who usually works under pressured mind set created by higher authority ? And the police never understand the definition of emotion. They only need proof - proof of living, proof of dying, proof of honesty. After collecting all the evidences why they put an innocent person in the dock as a criminal?

Papa, I cannot express in words how I controlled myself. I know you also have the same question as to why I didn't go to the police.

I will tell you exactly why I could not go to the police.

John's calls were coming continuously, he was now begging from me for 500 dollars. I continued talking him to see the real face behind all his crime which shattered me completely. The face with whom I had been talking since several months. The face with whom I got emotionally attached who filled up the loneliness of my life. That face who kept deceiving me, took advantage of my loneliness and robbed me and left me at the same point from where this circle of crime initiated. I will give you 500 dollars John only on one condition, just do a video call right now.

Papa and at that time there was no flight from Great Manchester to Mumbai.

Papa, he did not make video call at that time and said that I will definitely reveal about myself because you are a very pure soul, you have fed me.

There was a bustle in my mind, a storm, a pain; I had never thought that I would ever be cheated like this in my life. I wish you were with me today.

I controlled myself and considered it my moral responsibility to inform Dr. Naskoon. I wrote everything in his inbox of insta after all it was a violation of his privacy. They could have filed defamation case against him but those brothers did not take it seriously. They just messaged me, thank you for sharing the information. The Number of cyber crime have gone exponentially high because of such irresponsible people.

Papa, these people were educated doctors, didn't they have any responsibility? These two brothers came to Kerala; they were welcomed in Kerala as if God had come. These followers of other religions went to our temples, stood in front of the idols of God with folded hands, bowed their heads at the feet of the idols, I came to know all these things from the photos and reels posted on their Insta page. Surprisingly, after just two days they both removed all the photos and reels of their visit to India from instapage. Why didn't they remove any other photo? Why are they so welcomed in India and that too especially in Kerala? Is there a shortage of IVF doctors in India? Are the doctors here not that qualified? Are their chocolate faces influencing the women and girls of India?

Now I wanted answers to all my questions to get to the bottom of this matter. Papa, I inherited this trait from you only. I started giving likes to their instagram post. Their Posts were always about lectures on IVF and also showing child birth procedures .There was only a post on their Insta page about giving birth to children, looking at their post it seemed as if they had opened an entire hospital on this page showing the full process of child birth, how a child is born, how a test tube baby is born, what to eat, what to drink, when to have sex and how appropriate is sex during pregnancy, etc.

As I started liking the posts of these twin doctors of Turkey, surprisingly there was a flood of friend requests on my Insta page and Face book account too. The main focal point which driven my attention towards them was their relation to England and America, they all were doctors. First one who approached me on Instagram was George Paul, who was an orthopedic working in a hospital of Kosovo. He also requested to be a friend and he told that he belongs to California.

I asked why?

I liked your Photo on Instagram.

I scrolled his Insta page and found out that he had also opened a hospital on his Insta page, just like doctors of Turkey.

In order to unearth the mystery hiding behind their friend requests, I accepted few request from these doctors. Knowing the fact that I am not an extraordinary person, I was surprised that why these doctors are so eager to be friend with me.

I was utterly dumbfounded at John Rose's insolence that he was still asking $500 from me.

He was too overconfident to be caught that determined me to unfold the mask which he was wearing from the very beginning and shook my whole existence.

John told me that you will probably get scared after seeing my photo; you will never talk to me again.

If I don't talk, what difference will this make to you?

The impact on me is beyond your understanding said John.

Along with George Paul, I was also in conversation with other doctors too.

Doctor George Paul also refused to make a video call stating that the hospital doesn't allow the video call. I was very surprised why video calls are not allowed?

Pattern of discussion by Doctor George Paul was almost similar to John Rose specifying his marital status as unmarried and the only child of his parent owning number of properties in England. He has started liking me a lot, there were such ridiculous things but I was tolerating them because I wanted to know who these people are?

Along with George Paul, Dr. Greg Thomas, Dr. Ramesh Jovran were all talking to me. All of them were foreigners. Dr. Greg Thomas was a resident of America, he had a daughter named Sonia, she was studying in a boarding school of America, thankfully he was not a bachelor but he was divorced. He was also thirty-eight years old and was working in Kosovo too.

During our conversation, he was very keen to share his personal details with me even knowing only a little bit of my back ground. Without paying attention to my reply, in a very straight forward way, he kept proposal of marriage in front of me.

Before I could answer, he started telling me that he is fond of gardening, swimming, going to clubs, theatre, partying with friends, and traveling all over the world. If you marry me, you will get American citizenship and you will become a citizen of a powerful country? And you will get opportunity to travel whole world with me.

I kept one condition of making a video call before accepting his proposal .(I was handling all these fraudsters very cautiously as per Hindi Proverb- **DOODH KA JALA CHHACH BHI FOOK FOOK KAR PEETA HAI**)

Then he agreed to connect via video call after reaching home.

But you have to do me a favor darling?

What favor?

Because of my leave rejection I have not been able to meet my daughter since two years.

So how can I help you with this?

I will send you an email ID and also an account.

Okay.

You will have to write an email to this account and also transfer 2 dollar in the mentioned account.

What should I write in that email?

You have to write that you are the wife of Greg Thomas, please grant leave for him.

So anyone can write this, why me?

No, only relatives can write. I have neither parents nor any close relative.

If I write this, will they grant you leave?

Yes

But why two dollars?

This is the fee here.

All right then first do a video call?

After that will you do this work for me? I promise, I will take you around the world.

Okay, I am waiting for your video call.

I was wondering where these social platforms are driving all of us. Are these consequences of Advance Technology Papa?

It was 2 o'clock in the night; Greg Thomas did a video call.

Oh darling, why can't I see your face?

Because today here is electricity cut since morning at my place.

Well, don't you have back up?

No

Papa, I was trying to engage him in that conversation for some more time but he soon disconnected the video call saying that the network was not working properly.

After disconnecting video call he asked me for help?

I said of course but then do a video call one more time!

Don't you trust me?

Of course I do, but I want to know fully, who is desiring to get marry me.

Oh, that's it darling, he said and laughed mysteriously but papa, I didn't feel like laughing today because this time I could distinctly perceive the sly person hiding behind that charming and beautiful face.

No problem darling, I will call you later.

The second was Dr. Ramesh JoVran, who told about himself that his ancestors were residents of Pune (India) and had settled in England. That's why his name was Indian. Without asking, he also revealed his entire life history to me. He had two children, a twelve year old daughter and an eight year old son. His wife had left him and eloped with another man. The children were living with their grandmother in England and he too was working as physician in a hospital of Kosovo. Papa, you will not get surprised this time to know that he too proposed to me is now self explaining.

I was stunned to see his photo wearing only underpants. Which is called **JANGHIA** (underwear) in the rural language. It was too low on his waist that only a little pull would make him naked. For What purpose he was sending me these absurd pictures? Papa, you a being a man I don't feel the need to explain any further.

After sending this photo he asked me to comment on it?

Don't you have clothes to wear?

What do you mean?

I mean you should be suave enough to share decent pictures to a lady.

Controlling my anger I said, should I expect more shit then this from you?

Oh darling, do you even joke?

What does this even mean?

Meaning, you look like a very simple girl in the photo, no problem, I am sending you my good photo. Papa, he sent me several photos showing his family members son and daughter. His appearance was also very charming.

I also asked Dr. Ramesh Jovran to do a video call - he also gave the same rote answer that he is on duty at the moment and cannot call from the hospital. I will call you when reaches home at night.

I laughed out loud after hearing his answer.

He asked – Why are you laughing?

Nothing just like that.

Do you think I'm a trickster? He said angrily.

I didn't mean that.

I will call you in some time; I have to attend an emergency case.

That whole day gone, Papa, but Dr. Ramesh did not call me. Yes, the next day I got a call from Greg Thomas. Hey Papa, the same Greg Thomas who had asked for 2 dollar only. He talked to me on video call for about 2 minutes. While Conversation, I noticed his voice distinctly strange and my other suspicion was that he didn't blink his eyes at all. Even his facial muscles were rigid too, It seemed as if I was talking to stone faced man. Like a puppeteer performing his show, he speaks in the background and the puppets dance at his command with a string tied to his hand. His face was exactly the same. After some time, he said that I will call again tomorrow, darling now you write a mail to the American Embassy for my leave and also send 2 dollars and hung up the phone.

I got indulged in my thoughts. Suddenly I got diverted by doctor Ramesh jovran Video call. During two minutes conversation, he was sitting on his driving seat in his car and I was pretty sure that it was also a video app call. Repeating the same style where only his lips were moving, not his face. It seemed as if a puppet was speaking.

In order to help one of his friend residing In India, he asked me to give ten thousand rupees. And he also promised me to revert this money when he will visit to India. And tomorrow is my birthday, what gift are you giving?

What do you want darling, I asked?

For the first time I called someone darling.

I want only a gold chain; have heard that gold is very cheap in India.

How many grams of gold chain do you need?

Not much, just 50 grams.

How will I send you?

Do one thing Ramesh, you come to Delhi airport tomorrow, I will give you a gold chain of 100 grams. And we will also celebrate your birthday party together.

He understood that I was taunting him. He abused me badly and hung up the phone. On the other side, Greg Thomas kept pleading for 2 dollars. I still don't understand what will he do of these two dollars. John Rose kept asking me for 500 dollars saying this is last and today when he sent his real photo, I got scared after seeing his face. Terrible eyes stretched up to the ears like a black ghost. Very big hanging lips, wicked smile with white shinning teeth. Papa my mind got distorted after looking his fearsome face. Realizing the fact I was talking to this face I was almost fainted.

Then he called me, I picked up the phone, I was very scared, my voice was trembling while talking. Again I asked him to do a video call. Not now I will do some other time.

Why not now?

I'm very hungry right now, just give me 500 dollars. I promise you that I would show you my real face on video call.

Papa, although I was very scared, that night was very terrible for me, still I asked for a video call. I asked John is this your real name?

Yes darling now I will not lie to you. I am from South Africa. I also have a twin brother, Joel Rose. He is doing ward boy course.

So why did you use Dr. Naskun's face? How do you know them? And when you made a video call to me, how did you use Naskun's face while on video call.

Actually we talk through a video app.

What do you mean by this WE, I was dazed at this How many people are there in your gang?

No, I have done this work for the first time. Papa, I was listening silently. He told that he had worked in Naskun's clinic in Turkey; he used to do cleaning there. But they hate black people and they never paid me a salary. When I asked you for money for food, I was actually in the corridor of a very dirty hotel in Turkey. I will always be indebted to you for feeding me continuously for seven months. I will never forget that a woman, who knew my truth, still did not say anything to me. Saying all this he cried very loudly.

We both were silent for a while.

Breaking after a pause breaking this silence I asked how did you talk through a video app.

Have you heard about Artificial Intelligence?

Yes I know.

Simply through that we can create anyone's face and keep speaking ourselves from behind the scene. If you have noticed, when I used to talk with Naskun's face on, only my lips would be moving and there would be no expression on my face nor would my eyes blink. That's why I used to make a video call very quickly so that you won't be able to catch this deception.

That means you guys are misusing Artificial Intelligence?

I did it for the first time, but fraudsters are using it since long.

Where are these fraudsters from?

South Africa, Egypt, Nigeria and many more from India too.

From where in India?

He escaped this question very smartly.

If you had told me the truth before, I would not have felt bad.

Now after knowing the truth, are you helping me? Until you were not aware of truth, you kept sending me money because you loved Dr. Naskun's face, not me.

Saying this I will talk to you later, he hung up the phone.

Papa, I was forced to think about what he said, why was he so confident that I would still send him the money and not afraid of getting caught at all. Further he told me a lot about why those people were not afraid of being caught

On the other hand, Greg Thomas was asking me every day for 2 dollars but Dr. Romesh Jovran understood that I have judged his trap. Many doctors wanted to talk to me. Everyone had the same rote dialogues, almost the same.

Then another doctor named as Rayan Ahmed contacted me, the face on his profile was that of Ben Naskun, twin brother of Dr. Benton Naskun. During our first conversation when I told him directly that this is not your real face, at first he got scared but immediately he introduced himself. He told that he belongs to Egypt a very poor country and studying medicine course in America.

I am short of money can you send some money for my food and he abruptly asked do you believe in racism?

The people here do not like us because we are black, they misbehave with us. None of the professors and students in the medical college wants to talk to us properly.

After listening all this I asked him why did he used Naskun's photo on his insta profile?

Because everyone tends to get attracted towards beautiful and fair face, especially the girls and women of India and then after falling in fake love with these faces, they are biased to send money?

How did you ask for money from these girls?

I convinced these girls send money by saying that I am stuck somewhere and my wallet has been stolen.

Then ?

Then what, they send money to me?

Indian girls are really very nice and stupid too.

Papa, after hearing this, I got so angry that I want to slap him. These people are managing their living from here and are also making fun of us.

How many girls have been trapped by you till now using Naskun's photo?

I don't remember counting.

You are the first girl who is not an idiot.

What is your age?

I am 28 years old.

Aren't you afraid that you will be caught and may even go to jail?

He laughed saying that who will catch us, your police or your government?

Our People living in Delhi, Kerala and Bangalore are doing business of drugs and fake currency, have they been ever caught? There is a syndicate running fake currency of 500 rupee notes in your India, controlled by foreigners' tycoons. Can you identify whether the 500 rupee note kept in your purse is real or fake?

Papa, I was shocked at his frankness. I asked him to do a video call right now?

He immediately called and I got scared to see his horrifying face.

While hanging up the phone he said, I know you are very intelligent; you might be trying to trace this number by engaging me in talks for a long. But I am not a stupid.

Papa, I immediately dialed that number but the number was switched off. Don't know how many SIM cards these people keep and why they are not afraid of anyone?

I was continuously sending messages to Naskun Brothers about how these scammers are duping innocent women by using their beautiful and charming faces but ignoring this social responsibility those twin brothers were busy in advertising and promoting their clinic on instgarm and even they were not at all worried about their honor and respect.

They were not at all concerned that someone was getting ruined because of these people. They were engrossed in their own world.

Papa, now all the scammers were suddenly vanished from my Insta page except john Rose who was continuously begging for 500 dollars. I don't know why I was still talking to him? I just wanted to see his face once on video call. That face which, wearing the mask of Naskun shuddered me completely. All my principles collapsed and perhaps I myself had crushed my dignity under my own feet. Papa, what was my fault in this entire episode?

Without any fear and hesitation John Rose was continuously asking for 500 dollars. Surprisingly I noticed another storm of Indian girls and women asking for information about Naskun's Brother on my insta page. A sixteen year girl contacted me assuming that I Knew these Naskun's brother very well and i will be able to make them talk to these Naskun's brothers. She was madly in love with them that she wanted to Doctor Naskun by any means. This girl even sold her mother's jewellery and sent sixteen lakhs rupees to that Swindler. All of them were also trapped and looted in the same manner as I was. All of them were madly in love with those twin brother faces who unintentionally ignored this online honey tarp Scam. They were engrossed in their own world busy and enjoying with their families having beautiful wives and children unwitting about this scam happening around them.

Papa, I don't know how expanded this scam can be? But this seems to be a never ending trap. They will be the same dodger but will just keep changing their ways.

Now let me tell the story of those three women, one of them was the mother of two children, was thirty-five years old another was a widow having two kids.

She had also sent thirty-five lakh rupees to that scammer. And she was cheated and trapped in the love trap.

I am not writing their names here. She asked me to talk to Naskun's Brothers. I will be very grateful to you. After listening to her entire story, I tried to clarify to her that whoever spoke to you was not Ben Naskun, he was a swindler. Ben Naskun is married and is also the father of two beautiful girls. His wife is also very beautiful, why would he trap you in his love? And as far as I have been able to make out from them from their insta page, they look gentlemen and family oriented person. Some thug has made a video call with his face impersonating him. Papa, she was not ready to accept it. She believed that after seeing her, Ben Naskun would divorce his wife and marry her. I got tired of explaining to her, every day a message would come to me from her asking me to talk to Ben Naskun once. Finally I blocked her account. She was a resident of Maharashtra state.

Along with this, there was another lady, who was a gynecologist residing in Punjab also contacted me. Papa I will not tell you her name. She had two sons, her husband also worked in the same hospital.

They had a love marriage. Her elder son was sixteen years old and younger son was thirteen years old. She was 45 years old. One scammer had also approached her disguised himself as Ben Naskun. She did not suffer much loss; she lost only five lakh rupees. When her own bank account became empty, she stopped giving money. But she did not stop talking to that scammer, she started loving his voice. She explained herself as fatty and shapeless woman. The thug had advised her to join the gym to shed extra fat from her body so she will be the most beautiful lady in the world.

Following on the advice of that chiseler, this lady doctor started doing gym, every morning she would wake up and walk briskly for an hour. This woman herself told me that her husband always told her to go for a walk in the morning. He might have been saying this every day but she did not listen to him but at once agreed with the words of an unknown person, what kind of mania or delusion was this under which she was living and had tied herself in the love loop of that person. She had a love marriage and her husband was more handsome and smarter than Ben Naskun.

Despite explaining everything in detail to her, she was reluctant to accept this scam.

Yes, I know it very well, somehow I want to go to Turkey once and meet Ben Naskun. I have got Ben Naskun's mobile number, now he chats with me daily. And I also talk to that scammer because his voice inspires me to live happily.

You already knew so much and then what do you want from me? Will your husband not object or ask anything about this if you will go Turkey.

After reaching Turkey, I will marry Ben Naskun and will not return back.

I was shocked what forced you to tell me all this?

I am warning you so that you stop following and liking him, he is only mine. O characterless woman.

Papa, I had a very long conversation with this woman.

O CHARACTERLESS WOMAN!

Papa, these words of this educated woman kept resonating in my mind. Finally I blocked her number too.

But the flood of scammers continued on my Insta page. Papa, It is a never ending list and these letters would never be enough to narrate these incidences.

Papa, I could not understand this Indian doctor woman, when I blocked her on Instapage, then she contacted me again from a new account telling that she finds her father in Ben Naskun. When I overlooked her messages, she opened her third account and then kept stalking me until I stopped liking Naskun Brothers' posts.

An organization also contacted me saying that they want to talk to me about something very essential. When I ask, what is your introduction? Then he asked me to download Telegram app.

Why only Telegram app?

Because we talk only on Telegram app.

I said I don't know how to download the app.

It is very simple madam, go to Google Play and download it.

I said I will do it tomorrow.

He ended the conversation saying that I will contact you tomorrow at the same time.

This organization shared these conversations in the message box of my Insta page.

Surprisingly, all the impersonators had insisted to download Telegram app as a mode of conversation,

perhaps the conversations on it could not easily intercepted.

When I visited their profile of this organization, I got confused to see the profile photo of a man intentionally showing his back only. There was only one post on his insta page and that too was not clearly visible. Despite only one unclear post on this account suspiciously had five lakhs followers this drove me to get deep in to collect information from their followers account too.

There was no message for next three days. Life had started elapsing like a silent wheel. There was a poignant reminder of the passing time all around. It seemed as if a storm had passed blowing everything encircling around it.

Papa, I don't know how to gather my scattered thoughts.

Then after few days, there were two more messages on my Insta. One from the same organization and the other from a man named David Wilson. He told that he is a pilot in British Airways and wanted to be friend with me. When I visited his Insta page, there were four photos of a young and handsome man. **He had mentioned on his profile that he was a submarine Captain. I asked him, what do you want to say?**

I want to be friend with you; can you share your Whats App number?

No, I don't give my number to strangers.

Since I am talking to you, I am not a stranger any more.

So what?

If you are talking to me, then how are we strangers now?

Okay, then send me your number, I will call you right now.

He wrote down his number started with the same code which John Rose was calling from, papa it can't be a co-incidence that both relate to the same country.

I messaged David that I am doing a video call to you right now, please answer the call.

No-no darling, I am on duty at this time. I will definitely do a video call to you when I am free.

No David, I know you will never do a video call.

Why darling?

Because this number is fake and so are you.

Why? Do you work in any telecom company? He wrote irritably.

Because submarine captains do not fly airplanes.

Knowing that he landed on wrong platform he immediately blocked my account; obviously he must have also have abused.

Papa, one thing was common among all these fraudsters that age was just a number and every victim was DARLING to them. They all were smart swindlers who were changing their face every day.

Papa, now finally I would like to mention about that organization who also showed interest in talking to me on Telegram app only. He asked me on Insta, have you downloaded Telegram?

I answered NO. Who are you?

Actually our king wants to talk to you and he talks only on Telegram?

King! I asked who is your king and who are you? I was scared, papa.

No, don't worry, I mean the group leader.

Papa, I was surprised that he could sense my nervousness just by my words.

He wrote that our organization works for truth and our members are all over the world. If you become a member of our organization, you will never have shortage of wealth. But you will have to keep your identity secret as per the rules of our organization.

What does it mean to keep my identity confidential?

This is the rule of our organization.

What kind of rule is this? If your organization is doing good deeds, then what is the need of hiding the identities of the members involved in your organization?

Dear Madam, to accomplish true deeds one has to commit crimes too.

What? Then find some criminal, you are asking for wrong deeds from an innocent person.

Because this is what my leader wants, he is very impressed by your magnetic personality.

But you haven't revealed the name of your organization yet?

Illuminati, We all are committed to the **ILLUMINATI** organization.

As soon as I read the name of Illuminati, I blocked that account too.

Papa **Illuminat**i is such a mysterious organization of the world whose reality no one has been able to find out till date.

It is believed that Illuminati started in Bavaria City of Germany. In 1776, Professor Adam Wishapt of Ingolstadt University laid the foundation stone. Initially its name was Order of Illuminati. At that time, the fundamentalism of the Church and the Christian religion was deeply rooted in the society. To eliminate this imposed conservative fundamentalism, Professor Vishapatt started this organization. Through Illuminati, wanted to create a world without walls of religion and consistent equality among each other, still knowing the fact, government completely banned this organization.

But even today many people believe that Illuminati is still active and it is behind whatever is happening suspiciously in the world. Many people assumed that the Illuminati was responsible for the assassination of John F. Kennedy. There is a theory regarding Kennedy's death that at the time of assassination he was seen with some women carrying a gun like camera with them. These women are called The Babushka Ladies. It is believed that they were related to Illuminati. Even today the mystery of Illuminati has not been revealed and no one knows what his truth was. The symbol of this group is the eye of the owl, which is considered the goddess of knowledge. Many American celebs are suspected to be associated with this group. People of this group live a very mysterious life but from time to time they make their presence felt through some selected gestures. This mysterious society has many targets.

But why they approached me is still a mystery.

I was very scared but after that this group never contacted me again. I missed you a lot papa.

Finally One day John Rose connected with me via Video call. But the voice was not matching his face at all. Saying this now you have seen my real face again he asked for 500 dollar. This time all his facial movements were very clear confirming the reality of video call. Papa, his face was very horrifying.

It was a real video call with a real face. He was very hopeful that I would definitely give him 500 dollars after this call.

He asked me now will you give me 500 dollars?

Ignoring his question, I asked - Just tell me one last thing, how do you guys decide that this particular man or woman can give money.

At first he hesitated while telling but then he told that some bank employees keep on informing us in advance about their account details.

Employees of which banks?

Few Employees of all banks work for us on commission bases. This information explains these fraudsters fearlessness too. After taking names from there, we target those people who have Rs ten or fifteen lakhs in their account. We never target people having huge amount of money in their accounts.

Why is that John?

The person who is having huge amount is powerful. But sometimes we rob even very rich people thoroughly.

Don't they complain about you?

No |

Because these people think that it doesn't matter if the money is lost, the respect remains.

And have you guys ever thought about those who commit suicide?

No, this is not our Concern..

Then how do you find people like us?

All details like name and photo are provided by bank itself then we search those name Instagarm and Face book. We always target opposite sex victim. We have a vast network of people. One hand is joined to the other like a chain to accomplish this goal. **This is also called honey trap darling**. There are many other ways by which we rob people. You must now have fully understood this scam of Honey Trap. By the way, long live the internet and long live the cyber platforms. Saying this he laughed out a loud. Despite knowing this bitter truth I was looking at his face like an idiot and finding myself very helpless.

He then repeated his question: Will you still give me 500 dollar? He was a big bloody Bastard.

I said absolutely not.

He said that I knew this fact that you won't be able to complain about me. I told you all this because I'm really in love with you. For the first time, my mind scolded of deceiving you .Now I have confessed everything in front of you, hope you will forgive me. Although you loved Dr. Naskun's face very much but thank you very much for feeding me and taking me out of that dirty hotel corridor. Now I will never call you. Papa, saying this he blocked my number. Even today I look at the picture of Doctor Naskun like an idiot.

Papa ,I have written and dedicated this book remembering you and tried to collect a plethora of incidences and shattered feelings which are now dominating this world, I don't know whether these words will reach you or not but I got convinced by one of my well wisher named Shivam Sahani 's couplet -

Who says words don't go across?

Just pick up the pen with that solidity once.

Papa, toady I will not say the rest in next letter because I could feel that wetness in my heart flowing from your tears filled eyes.

Your Daughter Vedika

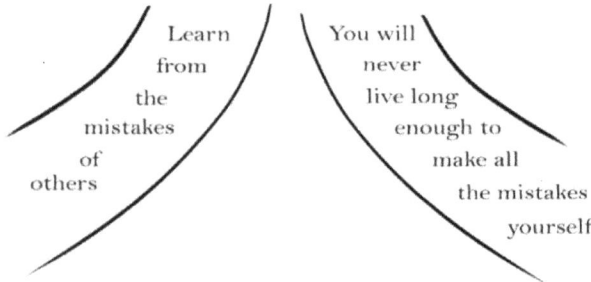

Grocho Marx who was an american comedian, writer & singer has said...

Learn from the mistakes of others / You will never live long enough to make all the mistakes yourself.

(This love story is not only vedikas only, any men and women having love emotions can connect to this story. Love is an unconditional element, which expands its dimension of impulses and emotions in anyone's heart. To fulfill this love one can sacrifice its whole life. This is vedika's story so I am narrating about her only. After facing this horrifying incident, there was a question in her eyes-"Am I Characterless?. I asked with surprise who all are saying this? She answered-"Many out there." I was surprised but I felt her anguish.

Vedika insisted me to pen her anecdote in my words. Since my father used to write very lengthy letters to me and she used to imagine those incidences happening in front of her eye by those conversation written in the letters. She wanted this story also to be written in the same way as my father used to write to me. She wished this story to be imprint on everyone's conscience. Now, she also felt the need to share her emotions with her father through her letters. I have attempted to write as she wished.)

Sudha Sikrawar

******

Epilogue

Conveying my thoughts through a story or writing a book was never new to me but when a story or incident t which had happened in one's life can throw light on different facets of our society become a foremost responsibility of any writer. This driven me to narrate and compile these incidences in this book.

This book has come to an end but story never ends here. With the advancement in technology, Modi ji's ambition of Digital India has taken cyber crime to a very high level. The world has gone crazy on Instagram and Other social platforms. Everyone is busy in posting the pictures of eating, drinking, dancing, singing, worshiping, changing their clothes and they doesn't even mind showcasing pictures of their bedrooms too. Each member of family is busy fidgeting with their mobiles and posting as well as watching the idiotic and nonsense reels without realizing its negative impact on body and mind. People have become distant from their loved ones in their own home and are trying to make the strangers their own.

And by taking advantages of this latest technology, few criminal minded and opportunistic rascals have spread their trap to target the innocent people. Social media platforms have now become such a place for business and plunder for scammers to drive of their Network conveniently sitting at their own place.

Shutting down of internet data for few minutes generate a robust restlessness around the world. Unintentionally we have become complete slaves of internet. We are passing through such a period of mental slavery, which we ourselves are not aware of. Internet has become such a wheel on which we all are spinning in a never ending loop like idiots.

If we talk about medical science, one of the diseases is Down syndrome. This is a genetic disorder caused by extra genetic material from chromosome 21 due to abnormal cell division. Treatment may be beneficial but it cannot be cured. Today we all are afflicted of this Down syndrome of the Internet. We can call it also afflicted Syndrome of internet.

This is really surprising that why do Indian girls and married women feel the need for this foreign internet love? Are they underdog of negligence from their own people? Despite having everything, why are they attracted towards materialism? I agree that loneliness can force a person towards wrong path and such corridors of our lives will ever dominate destroying our self-esteem, is beyond my imagination?

I told Vedika that let's report to the police. She declined immediately saying that there is no use. Vedika had a very open conversation with John Rose; she firmly believed that they run a very strong network of scammers to conclude these robberies. And these robbers had the entire organization under their control.

Another Important Concern of Vedika was that she could be exposed because of her intimate messages sent to John Rose.

Some people do not file a complaint out of shame and some do not go to the POLICE to avoid the strange attitude of police towards them. I was wondering why only women are becoming victims of this honey trap? Indian men do not give love that to them or is this a mere attraction towards these foreign chocolate faces? But my illusion was smashed when the grandfather of another acquaintance of mine became a victim of this honey trap too. He was seventy years old, his wife had died two years back and other family members was engrossed in their own world leaving him alone at home. To abolish his loneliness, he started using social media platform and ended up becoming a victim by a female. Then one day a foreign girl talked to him on video call. A series of intimate talks continued and then one day the foreign girl took off all her clothes and danced in front of him on video. Eventually he also got carried away and took off his clothes too. He was seduced not because he was a man rather he was alone. He was a stranger in that crowded house surrounded by his own people.

That girl took a photo of him dancing in naked position and made a video reel too. Then she started blackmailing him, saying that she will circulate this video on social media. He got scared, he had Rs 10 lakh in his account, and he had to give it all. The money ended but the process of black mailing did not end. At this point having numerous suicidal thought, he finally shared everything to his granddaughter of twenty-two years old. His granddaughter talked to that foreign girl and said that you can easily make my grandfather's photo viral on social media. It will not effect upon us as we all remain naked at home and so do our neighbors. After applying this trick the process of black mailing stopped. This Incident emphasis on the fact that how crucial is it for someone to be close with you? That granddaughter supported her grandfather instead of criticizing him, only then he was able to come out of that problem.

Again I tried to mentally prepare Vedika to file a complaint against that scammer. Then news of female police officer becoming victim of this trap went viral on the social media. Sixty lakhs were looted from her. The first lesson taught in police training is to have doubt. These people reach up to any conclusion only on the basis of doubt. But here why did she not have any doubt because her mind was captured in the spider's web or in web of love? Then almost every day I was reading and listening news of these victims and scams. The faces of the defrauder were hidden. There was a flood of frauds by which everyone got swept away. Teachers, officers, doctors, scientists, no one could escaped.

Many people committed suicide and many lost their jobs just because of these honey trap and scams.

Hardly two or three percent go to the police to complain. Because our legal system is very debilitated and very slow.

When cases like rape and murder take years to get justice, then how will the law punish these cyber criminals who are already bonded with officials of bank? Despite prevalence of these cyber crimes around the world neither the police nor the law is getting affected. The process of getting justice is so slow that sometimes even the fourth generation gets justice and that generation is not even aware of the crime as well as the justice. Why should they suffer the deeds of his ancestors?

But in all these situations we too are responsible somewhere. Staying at home and not talking to each other, we are creating love stories and weaving dreams with strangers.

Today is the era where everyone demands his/her own space in their lives. By taking advantage of today's living style, these scammers are able to invade our privacy.

Social media platform is now a nuclear bomb, the day it explodes everything will be destroyed, and this can be reversible by awaking awareness and applying stringent laws.

I wonder why everyone needs this personal space today. Earlier, in our ancient system of united families, all members used to live in a single room of a house, laughing and holding each other's hand making a strong fist which could bear any pressures of surroundings circumstances. Today there are four rooms and two members living in them. We are so open and exposed on social media platforms that everyone can even read lines on our hand. Our past, present and future has become an open book and easily accessible by scammers on these platforms.

It is mandatory to halt and rethink that by abandoning the precious lifestyle given by our ancestors and accepting new technology in the name of development is creating loneliness in our lives.

A human life travels through various corridors to reach its destined end. But I never imagined that passing through these corridors of diverse emotions like love, hatred, deceive, jealousy and insecurity could also result in these amplified cyber crime of modern technology and digital India.

It is not necessary that we first make mistakes and then learn.

GROCHO MARX, who was an American comedian, writer and singer, has said –

Learn from the mistakes of others, you will never live long enough to make all the mistakes yourself.

Sudha Sikrawar

******

At last some lines about "me"

When the existence of "I" always direct our life then how an author can remain untouched by this" I". It is unlikely that I will be able to write a book like this in future again. While writing, I of any writer is always present somewhere in it. In this, it was not only me but my father was also present with me, who no longer alive while writing this book, I felt as if he was sitting in front of me. Just like in my childhood I used to sit in front of him with my entire questionnaire. I used to ask a flurry of questions and always got satisfying answers from him. Although I was writing this letter to Vedika's father thinking that if my father would have been there how he have dealt with these situations. It was very difficult for me to write this book. At last I finished this book on my part yet it will never be complete.

Sudha Sikrawar

I am ending this story with heavy heart by quoting these lines from Shivam Sahani-

The heart still cries sitting below

The brain

The mind still says that you were forbidden

Not to love stones.

******

Vedika is a very dear friend of mine but I never dare to ask her what is in her heart because her eyes are always full of tears, which never shed, pierce my heart too.

For all the Readers

Perhaps you readers might feel that Vedika is displaying her stupidity by writing the truth about her. But it is also significant that how many people are there who are doing and have already done stupid things and became victims while reading this book? But maybe they don't have the courage to put their point forward in front of everyone bravely? I also realize that this story may also fall victim to severe criticism. But in some cases, the most intellectual people also became victim and looted like army officers, police officers, DRDO, bank officers, Software Engineers etc.

While criticizing this story, please keep these intelligent people in your mind too.

Sudha Sikrawar

Author Introduction

Name : **Sudha Sikrawar**

Father's Name : **Doctor Suraj Pal Sikrawar**

Education : **Post Graduate in Hindi**

Birth Place : **Palia Kalan Lakeempur Kheeri (U.P.)**

My Work -

Story : **Chaand Sanwla hai (Hindi Version)**

Threshold (English Version Of : **Chaand Sanwla hai)**

Poetry Collection : **Vihangini** (First Poetry Collection in Hindi) : **Parichita** (Second Poetry Collection in Hindi)

Crime Thriller : **Babu Mam Ki Vah Dusri Gali** (Hindi Crime Thriller)

That Second Street of Babu Mam (English Version)

First Article : **Published and awarded in Swatantra Bharat News Paper on the Dowry System at the age of eight.**

First poem : "*क्या खोज रहे हो तुम?*", published in Kadambini literary Magazine

First Story : *कमली*, Published in Kadmbini Literary Magazine

Other Stories : **Published In PUSHPGANDHA a literary Magazine of Ambala**

Upcoming Creations : Arnima And Kuch Khat Gazaala ke Naam

www.ingramcontent.com/pod-product-compliance
Lightning Source LLC
LaVergne TN
LVHW061618070526
838199LV00078B/7331